NATALIE'S CHOICE

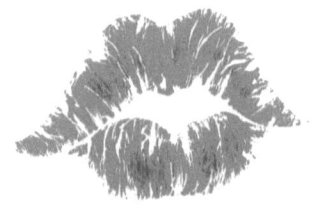

EVERNIGHT PUBLISHING ®

www.evernightpublishing.com

NATALIE'S CHOICE

NATALIE'S CHOICE

Chaos Bleeds, 10

Sam Crescent

Copyright © 2018

Chapter One

"Do you know what I realized every time I'm here?" Lacey asked.

"I have no idea." Natalie Pritchard smiled at Lacey in the mirror as she continued to run a brush through her hair.

"That you girls always get me to color your hair. I'm like the hair fairy or something."

She burst out laughing. "I was sitting outside and you dragged me in here."

"For a good cause," Lexie said. "Your hair was starting to look really unkempt and kind of, you know …"

"Gross," Lola said. "When was the last time you brushed it?"

Natalie stared at the old ladies of The Skulls MC that had decided to visit Piston County, along with the ladies who were her best friends of the Chaos Bleeds

MC. She never thought she'd actually be friends with a bunch of bikers' chicks, but here she was, getting her hair done while some of the women enjoyed some bubbly. Holding her cup, she'd not even taken a sip.

She never drank.

Most of the time she was the driver, seeing as Devil had helped her to pass her test in the past few months. She'd never had the time in high school. Between studying, her art, and the ranch, driving seemed pointless.

Of course, now that she was all alone, she didn't have much choice in the matter. Devil had been amazingly patient with her, taking his time to guide her. Out of all of the Chaos Bleeds men, he'd been the only one willing to give her a chance. All of the others had been terrified.

Poor Devil. During the first few lessons she nearly killed him.

"Remember you're carrying a father right now, and imagine that not only do my kids need me, but also the whole of the club needs me as well."

He'd often repeat those words, or some variation of those words. After the first few hiccups. everything was fine. Devil was alive and would be happy with his children—who she happened to babysit, or at least work as their live-in nanny.

"Your hair is perfect. Ignore them. You only had a couple of knots. Nothing I couldn't handle," Lacey said, patting her shoulder.

She liked Lacey. The woman was kickass, smart, and she didn't take any shit from anyone. Completely the opposite of her. She had a tendency to run and hide, or to accept the gibes that always came her way. High school had been the worst years of her life.

Still, she'd go through it all again if it meant

she'd get to be sitting here, talking with these amazing ladies.

All of them had curves, and all of them had men who were completely devoted to them, and she … no, she didn't crave it. She thought of both Butler and Slash, and she closed up, refusing to wish for something she'd never have.

"So, I hear you've not only got one man panting after you, but two," Lacey said.

"You should see Slash and Butler around her. Seriously, they're like two dogs chasing after their bone," Judi said.

Judi was married to Ripper and they had three beautiful babies. She was also Devil's adopted daughter, but she didn't know all the details related to Judi's adoption, only that she'd been a lot older than most kids, and had a really rough time of it.

"I bet they consider you a very tasty bone," Lacey said.

She chuckled. Slash and Butler.

Both men were gorgeous in their own way. Slash was … rock-hard, solid. He'd been to hell and back, and still managed to have a cheeky smile that was infectious. Butler was a different matter. He'd been an addict—his vice being drugs—but in recent years he'd also stopped drinking. There were many times she'd see him holding a bottle or a glass, but it always turned out to be a soda of some kind. He simply held it in a way that made it look like alcohol, just to fit in.

Slash had kissed her.

Butler didn't make her feel weird. He made her laugh by his blaringly obvious statements that were never designed to hurt. After her father's passing, she needed someone to say something like, "I know you're going through shit right now, but even though I sound like an asshole for saying it, it'll get better." Butler had been the one to say it. He'd not coddled her either.

Working on a ranch nearly every single hour of the day, being coddled or told everything was going to be all right, wasn't something she was used to. When Slash did it, she always felt like something was about to go wrong. Then there were times that she loved his optimism and she enjoyed his company. The kiss they shared had also been ... amazing. Her first kiss. Her only kiss.

Being a little older than Lola, she was still a virgin.

Yeah, in this day and age, she still held her precious V-card, and hadn't let it go. She took a sip of her drink.

"Both of those men are mighty fine. If you want to get away from it all though, there's always a place for you at Fort Wills, just so you know," Lacey said.

She smiled. "Thank you."

"A lady needs to realize that she's never alone. We're all together. Don't get me wrong, some of us really don't get along, but we deal with each other, and move on. We're a family, honey, and you're part of that."

Lexie moved toward her, wrapping an arm around her shoulders. "Just like you're part of our family."

She smiled, giving Lexie's arm a squeeze. Working for the Chaos Bleeds old women was a dream come true. Not only did she babysit or nanny for them, she helped to design and create their fashion line, which had amazing success online and in their store in town.

"You're all done. We've got to give it about an hour, and then we can wash it off," Lacey said, moving toward the next person.

She loved it when The Skulls women came. Everything just always felt so right, so together.

Natalie stayed in her chair and watched as Lacey made the rounds, doing some touch-ups followed by a few haircuts. When the time came to wash out the color, she was excited and nervous.

Lacey wouldn't let her look until she'd dried and styled it, and finally when she looked in the mirror, she loved it.

"I know some would complain that it looks like a unicorn, but this is so you."

"I love it," she said, spinning around and hugging Lacey tightly. Most of her hair was blonde, but when the length got to about her neck, the color changed from blonde to purple, to blue, then to red, with the tips being a lime green. She adored it.

"I figured the style made you look like your artistic self."

She gave a little twirl in the mirror.

"We're all heading back to the clubhouse now where they're finally going to serve some food. You coming?" Lacey asked.

"Yes." Her stomach growled and Lacey laughed.

"Tell me about it. I'm so starved right now. Cutting and styling hair always makes me hungry. Fucking, as well."

Natalie didn't say anything. She followed the women outside to the waiting cars. Dick, Ripper, and Death were the designated drivers it would seem. She climbed into the car with Judi, Lexie, and the kids, holding Laurell in her lap. Lexie and Devil's youngest, Amelia, was already strapped in her seat as well as David. Devil already had Simon, Elizabeth, and Josh back at the clubhouse.

Devil and Lexie had so many kids, six in total,

seven with Judi.

Every single day she saw the love, that sparkle between Lexie and Devil, though. Their love was ... it was like a fairy tale. No matter how many times Devil saw Lexie, Natalie always saw the look in his eyes. It was a mixture of love and lust that seemed to transcend all other emotion.

Conversation went on around her, but she didn't mind not joining in. It wasn't often that she had the confidence to actually be part of it.

Arriving at the clubhouse, she saw that it was really busy. The music seemed to vibrate, and she saw the excitement and happiness within the club. Climbing out of the car, Devil was already there to take his kids.

"Go and have fun." He didn't even look her way, taking his child, and helping his woman. She didn't linger, making her way into the clubhouse. Slash was the first person she encountered. Ever since they shared a kiss, or at least he kissed her, and she didn't respond, he made her a little nervous. Not uncomfortably so, just ... there.

"Hey," she said.

"Wow." He stared at her hair.

She gave him a little twirl. "What do you think?"

"It's different. You were fine the way you were."

Natalie kept a smile on her face and nodded. One of the club whores that still stuck around wrapped her arms around Slash, and Natalie used it as a chance to escape. Couldn't he have said something nice?

"Well, damn, I'll certainly see you in a crowded room," Butler said as she made her way outside. He stepped toward her, holding her hand, and making her give a twirl. "Sexy as fuck."

Why couldn't Slash do that?

****

"Get the fuck off me," Slash said, pushing the bitch away.

"You know that's not a nice way to treat a lady," Lacey said.

He closed his eyes, counted to ten, and opened them to finally see the woman in front of him. Out of all of The Skulls women, he didn't like Lacey. She had an attitude that often rivaled Tate's and that was saying something.

"It's none of your business how I deal with bitches I don't want hanging over me."

"I wasn't talking about the club pussy. She's not here to be treated nicely. She likes giving it to anyone who'll pay her attention. That's a slut's way. No, I'm talking about Natalie. Couldn't you have said something nice to her?"

"Her hair was perfect the way it was. She didn't need to change it." She was sexy no matter what.

Lacey sighed. "You know, it amazes me at times how the world keeps on turning, and overpopulation could be a real threat seeing as men can't seem to get their heads out of their asses. It doesn't matter that she didn't need to change it. She wanted a change, and you know what, asshole, women like that feeling after having their hair done. The one that makes them feel a little different, like a woman, ready to face the world, and shit like that. Ugh! You know what, let Butler have her. You're wasted on someone like Natalie."

She pointed somewhere behind her, and he quickly turned to see Butler holding Natalie's hand, and she was smiling.

Shit!

No, this was not happening.

Stepping outside, he watched as Butler pulled her into his arms, and then tilted her back as if they'd come to the end of the dance.

The moment Natalie caught sight of him, however, her smile died in her eyes, and it served him fucking right.

"I think your hair is nice," he said.

Again, she didn't smile.

"Nice? It's sexy as fuck, babe," Butler said.

"You're sexy, Natalie, no matter what color your hair is."

She didn't smile at either of them. Instead, she pulled away from Butler and made her excuses.

"You know, you don't know how to give a girl a compliment," Butler said. "She's clearly having a hard time of it, so she's doing something that makes her happy, and you're shitting all over it."

"Don't you think it's important for us to find out what the fuck the problem is?" Slash asked. "She dyes her hair today. What about in a week? Cutting herself? Taking drugs?"

Butler sighed. "You overthink everything, which I thought was hard to do without a fucking brain."

"Bite me."

"I would, but I'd go for your neck and get rid of my competition." Butler showed his teeth, and Slash walked away. He didn't want to pound Butler's face, especially as families were here, and it wouldn't be nice.

Natalie sat at one of the tables with all the kids. Ever since she'd been working for Lexie and Devil, she seemed to always gravitate toward the kids now. He didn't like that. She distanced herself at every single opportunity. He'd kissed her, and she'd withdrawn from him, but this had come a long time before he kissed her. She was part of them, but again, she wasn't.

Simon teased one of her curls, and he watched as she laughed. Eva, Tiny, and their kids were not here, so

Simon was in a sulk. Devil's son had a thing for Tiny's daughter, Tabitha. When the two were together, they were inseparable.

"Do you want to wipe up the drool?" Jessica asked.

She was a nurse and worked at the local hospital. In recent months, she'd begun to take time off, and he knew it was because Snake and Jessica were trying for a baby.

"It's not that bad." He still wiped his mouth though.

"Please. You're like a little puppy dog with the way you look at her."

From the first moment he saw Natalie he'd been smitten. She wasn't like any of the women at the club, or the old ladies, either.

The jeans she wore hugged every single curve, highlighting her rounded hips, and thighs made to be wrapped around him. He loved how gentle she was and had spent hours simply watching her sketch.

Not only did she design clothes, she also loved to draw and paint.

He loved quite a few of her pictures, and even had one on his wall, which reminded him constantly of her.

"You've not gotten very far with her, have you?" Jessica asked.

The kiss they shared meant something to him, but he also knew it had only served to put a distance between them. Not only that, Butler making her aware of their feelings pretty much screwed whatever friendship they had.

"She wants nothing to do with us," he said.

"So? You like her and she likes you."

"It's not the same." He watched as Natalie took

the pen Paul, Ripper and Judi's son, gave her, and began to add to the picture they were drawing.

"Please. I can't believe I'm hearing this bullshit. Between you and Butler, you're both fucking suckers. You're a Chaos Bleeds guy, and she's right there for you." Jessica rolled her eyes.

He was about to tell her to fuck off when Snake appeared. "My woman giving you a hard time?"

"No," Jessica said.

"Yes. Take her away before I find a reason to throttle her."

"You wouldn't do that, Slash." She winked at him and he shook his head as she walked away.

Heading to the table with the kids, he took a seat. "Hey, Slash," Simon said.

"You okay, bud?"

"Yeah, yeah." Simon stared across the backyard looking so fucking miserable.

"He's missing Tabitha," Natalie said.

"She said she was going to be here, and then her dad decided they needed to go to Vegas to see her granddad. Why couldn't Ned come here?"

"I don't think Ned and your dad get on all that well."

Simon scowled, got to his feet, and walked away.

It scared Slash how fast that kid was growing up. To him it didn't seem that long ago that they arrived in Piston County with the intention of finding Devil's kid and being on their way. Of course, the moment they hit the town, everything had changed.

Life had turned upside down, back to front, and been all over the place. Each step had brought him to where he was now. Staring across the table as Natalie tucked her multi-colored hair behind her ear.

She looked sexy as fuck, but he'd also seen her in

that dress she designed for herself, and knew she was perfect.

Being around the kids, he kept his needs in check, but it was driving him crazy pretending not to want her.

One of the kid's favorite songs started up, and they all left the table to head into the center of the yard and start dancing. Slash didn't want to lose an opportunity to dance with Natalie, and he saw her alone so he headed on over to her.

"Do you want to teach them how it's done?" he asked.

She burst out laughing. "I don't dance."

He held his hand out. "Come on, there's never a time when it's too late to learn."

Natalie nibbled her lip, and all he wanted to do was pull that lip out of her mouth and kiss the fuck out of her.

"I don't know."

"It's a dance. I'm a grown-ass man, Natalie. I'm not going to think you're offering me anything. It doesn't matter. I know you, and I know we're only friends." For now. "I just want to dance."

He saw the temptation there, and she finally relented, taking his hand.

Leading her onto the grass that others were dancing on, he kept hold of her hands, and started to sway.

"Isn't this a little childish?" she asked, as they followed the kids' moves.

"You've got to start somewhere. Did you ever go to a dance growing up?"

"No, not at all."

"Then this is one hell of a great start. You see, you sway from side to side when you're kids. Boys don't want to get close to girls. They've got weird diseases.

They like hugging, and being all gross, and boys can't be like that. We've got to be cool, you know. Nothing can bother us. We're in control."

She burst out laughing.

"Okay, so we're swaying."

"Yep, then there's a few cool moves." He spun her around a couple of times, and they did some action with their feet, shaking their hips as they did. Her smile was infectious as she copied him move for move.

"You ready to go up a level?" he asked.

"Sure."

His hand caught her hip and pulled her close.

"This is just going up a level?" she asked.

"Yes. You see, guys go from hating girls, to suddenly realizing there's a whole lot more to them. Everything suddenly seems like a lot of fun." He didn't cross any line or make her aware of the fact his cock was so hard it would push straight through his jeans. He simply held her close. To him, it was perfect.

****

"I have to wonder if you're even interested in Natalie," Jessica asked.

Butler turned his gaze from the dancefloor to look at Jessica. "And why would that be?"

"You're not trying to get in between them."

"I'm not going to be a child to get what I want."

"Is she who you really want? Slash loves her. You can see that clearly. You, you strike me as if you're waiting to cause some trouble."

"When I need your opinion I'll ask for it."

"Okay." Jessica held her hands up and stepped away. He kept on staring at her until she was far enough from him.

Turning, Butler looked directly at Natalie as she laughed at something Slash said. He wanted her, there was no doubt about that. But every time he wanted something, he was never half-assed with anything.

His addictions set him on a course, and the only reason he held back was purely because Natalie had been through enough. The last thing he wanted to do was scare her off or hurt her.

Running a hand down his face, he watched as Slash changed the dancing, and suddenly he held her close.

Natalie stared up at Slash, nervous, unsure, and he couldn't take it anymore. Stepping onto the dance floor, he moved right up behind her, placing his hands on her waist.

"Didn't anyone tell you that I know how to dance?" he asked, pulling her back against him. Slash, being the idiot that he was, let her go, and she was against his chest.

The scent of her surrounded him, and Butler felt that panic slowly ease away from him. With her in his arms, focus came back, and with it, a need unlike anything he'd ever known. Not for the drugs. No, it was a need to be this woman's everything.

No one else had seen through the bullshit lies she gave about feeling fine. Not one other member had seen that she wanted to sell her father's ranch. Slash himself had told her everything would be okay, and they'd help her out. He'd not seen that Natalie was slowly dying inside trying to keep a legacy alive that wasn't her own. He spun her around so that she was facing him.

"I love your hair," he said, watching her smile again.

"Lacey is amazing."

He ran his fingers down the strands, liking even more that she'd kept it down, and it wasn't trapped up in a ponytail. There were times he wondered if she even realized she was a woman.

"She really is." Not half as amazing as the woman in his arms.

Everyone was wrong about him. He wasn't trying to piss Slash off, or cause a problem. Natalie was unlike any woman he'd ever known. She wasn't after anything for herself. She was kind, sweet, charming, and so talented. Sitting with her, they could be in complete silence, or even talk about putting the world to rights. To him, it didn't matter. He just loved her company, and there's no way he's letting her go without a fight.

Chapter Two

Natalie finished packing the last of the pancakes with sprinkles she was trying out. The cookbook lay open with a little note from Simon asking if he could have them. She checked with Lexie last night before attempting to make them. Taking a bite of the weird one that always screwed up in the pan, she dipped it into the maple syrup she had keeping warm, and closed her eyes at the taste.

So nice.

"So, the hair? Is that a thing?"

Opening her eyes, she turned to see Devil standing in a pair of pajama bottoms, and nothing else, not even slippers. She herself wore pajama shorts and a cropped vest. Devil never leered at her, or even stared at her hair.

In fact, every time she saw him around other women, he rarely appraised them. Until Lexie came into the room, and, of course, his gaze followed that woman everywhere. Devil was a good-looking man, even with all of his ink that held the declaration of his love for Lexie and the kids. The list had grown a lot since Simon and Lexie's name, since they had more kids now.

"Lacey said she could give me something a bit different and I told her to have at it." She held the end of one of her new multi-color strands. "I like it."

"It suits you, I have to say. You even look happier for it."

She smiled. "It's nice." She ran her fingers through her hair and placed the pancakes in the heated oven to keep warm until all the kids woke up. Taking a seat at the kitchen counter, she sipped at her coffee, feeling Devil staring at her.

Glancing up at her, she discovered he was.

"Have I done something wrong?"

"Nope, you're fine. Slash and Butler."

Instantly she felt uncomfortable. They'd danced for about half an hour at the party last night, and she'd been so nervous. The club had been watching them, and even though she wanted to pull away, she'd not done it. Instead, she'd danced until Devil took over, dancing with her, and forcing the other men away. "Thank you for, you know…"

"Rescuing you?" Devil asked.

She nodded. "I didn't… I'm not trying to come between the club or anything."

"Believe it or not, Natalie, I know you're not. You looked nervous as fuck, and to be honest, if it hadn't been for Lexie asking me to save you, I wouldn't have. I'm not always going to be there to put a stop to it. I'm not going to treat you with kid gloves. Both of those men want a piece of you. That is going to cause a problem in my club no matter which way I look at it."

"Would you like me to leave town?" she asked, feeling the tears begin to build.

"No, I don't want that. I want you to realize you're going to have to make a choice."

"And if I don't make one?"

Devil's fingers tapped against the side of his cup, and stared at her. "Do you have feelings for either of them?"

"They're my friends, or at least I thought they were. When their feelings came out, I just stopped hanging around them. I didn't want to be cruel because I'm not ready for anything like that."

"I don't think you're a cruel woman, Natalie. Just be careful with my boys' hearts, okay? Butler's been through a lot, and as a whole, so has Slash. We've survived a lot of hard shit. We don't want or need any more."

"I won't. I promise."

She was saved from the conversation by Simon, Elizabeth, and Josh entering the room. Simon also carried baby Laurell in his arms.

"Dad, she needs changing, she totally stinks of poo."

Devil sighed. "I take it your mother has David and Amelia?"

"David had a bad dream about killer clowns, and was such a baby," Elizabeth said. "Simon said that was going to be his costume."

"Yeah, did Simon say if he asked his dad or not?" Devil asked.

"Come on, Dad, it's going to be Halloween."

"Would you wear it if I say we're heading to Fort Wills for a party and that Tabitha is dressing up as a princess?"

Natalie smiled as she saw Simon's interest perk right up. That boy was totally smitten with The Skulls girl. Natalie didn't want to leave until she watched how that played out. Even when they were kids, they were always sneaking cell phones to talk to each other. It was the cutest long-distance romance she'd ever seen.

"Are we?"

"Would you like to take that risk?"

"Tabitha's not afraid of clowns."

"That's where you're wrong." Devil stared at his son. "An easy way to settle this." Devil grabbed the phone and began to dial, pressing the button again for it to go to speaker.

"Hello," Tiny said.

"Tiny, is Tabitha afraid of clowns?" Devil asked.

"That's a weird question."

"Is she?"

"Tabitha, honey, what do you think of clowns?" Tiny asked.

"Why?" Tabitha asked.

"Devil wants to know."

"Tell him not to come as one. I told Simon years ago that I hated them, and he even punched a clown that was at the fair because he stood too close. Doesn't he remember?"

Devil gave Simon a pointed look. "That will be all." He hung up his cell phone. "Think about what you say to your brother before bed."

"I'll throw the costume in the trash," Simon said.

Natalie got the pancakes out of the oven, and began serving to the kids. "You'll do no such thing. I stitched that costume for you, and I won't have that fabric go to waste. If you give it back to me, I'll create something else."

"You even got Natalie to work for you?" Devil asked.

"I'm doing the dishes for an entire year, and she even makes sure to use as many pans as she can. She browns meat in one pan, fries onions in another," Simon said.

"Don't exaggerate." She rolled her eyes. It was one day that he was being a really bratty kid, and so she made him do a lot of dishes. He didn't complain while eating the food. "I'm heading into town later to go to the post office. I'm expecting a delivery of fabric, and I want to be there when it arrives. The company I ordered from has a history of getting orders wrong, and I don't want them to mess it up."

"Do you want me to come with you?" Devil asked. "Or get one of the guys?"

"I can go," Simon said. "I've got a letter I want to

mail."

There was no need to ask who the letter was for. Simon and Tabitha were also pen pals. She'd caught him writing so many letters over the past few months.

"I'm happy to take him," she said.

"Great."

Lexie walked in, and she watched Devil's eyes literally light up as she did. She was dressed in a sunshine yellow dress with matching flip-flops. In her arms she carried Amelia, and David walked beside her. His cheeks were red.

"Pancakes." She made to pass Devil, but he caught her around the waist. Natalie grabbed Amelia, kissing her cheek as Devil took his wife's lips.

"Morning, wife," he said.

All of the kids groaned around the table as if it was the grossest thing they'd ever seen, which always made her smile.

One day, she hoped to have a man like Devil who would love her so completely that all she had to do was walk into a room to brighten up his world.

They finished breakfast, and by the time she changed, Simon was already in the car, dressed, and ready to go.

"You never move this fast when I have to take you to school," she said, climbing behind the wheel.

"Well, duh, school is boring."

She knew from past conversations that Simon went every single day because his dad told him the only way to get a girl like Tabitha was to have a good education and a good brain.

Simon would do anything to make Tabitha happy.

Pulling out of the drive, she began her journey to town. "I've got to head to the supermarket first," she said.

"Sure, I don't mind. I've got nothing to do today." He rolled down his window. It was already hot, and the car was boiling.

The drive didn't take long, and Simon walked beside her as she got a cart and entered the supermarket.

"Does Dad know that you send stuff to Lucius?" Simon asked.

She paused, looking at Simon. Lucius was the man from the Chaos Bleeds: Nomad Chapter. She met him when his best friend Roxy had been dying, and she'd stayed in Piston County during her final days.

Before he'd left, he'd kissed her, but only to try to get the men to fight him. He'd wanted pain, and tried to do whatever he could to get it. A few days after he left, she got a text message, apologizing.

They talked, and whenever he needed something, she always sent him a care package in the general direction of where he was. He'd told her he would never settle down, that traveling and being on the open road was in his blood.

"I don't know." Lucius asked her not to tell Devil where he was, so she never did. It wasn't her business or her secret. However, now that Simon mentioned it, she felt so guilty.

****

Slash wasn't interested in any of the pussy that flashed his way. He sat at the table in Naked Fantasies, the nightclub owned by Chaos Bleeds. There were a couple of new women, and he saw several of the brothers wanting a taste, but he wasn't interested. He'd not been interested in free pussy for a very long time.

"What's wrong with you?" Dime asked, taking a seat at the bar. "You never check out the good pussy anymore."

"Didn't you hear? He's in love with Natalie,"

Charlie said, taking the seat on the other side of him.

Dime, Guts, Sexy, and Smithy were club members who hadn't fallen for any woman. They tended to taste all the free pussy now that a great deal of the club was already taken. There was also Wild and Bob. They were two prospects that earned their patch a few years ago.

Over the past few months, prospects had come and gone, never able to hack it for longer than a couple of weeks, thinking it was something easy to be part of. Slash believed it was because of that popular TV show—that he hadn't seen—but Natalie had gotten him a t-shirt, which he'd thought was fucking cute.

"Aw, are you going to get married and have lots of babies?" Sexy said.

"Fuck you."

Just then one of the women approached. She had that sway in the hips that told them she was looking for some action. Dime was the first to reach for her, pulling her into his lap.

"Hey, boys, I'm bored," she said.

"Now, Dolly, how could you possibly be bored when you've got all the men that you'll ever need right here?" Dime stroked her thigh. She wore a garter belt with a corset. Her tits bulged out of her top.

To a lot of men, she was the epitome of sex and beauty. All he wanted was a cute, sexy-as-fuck tomboy who liked to wear jeans. Who stared in the mirror looking scared at the mere sight of a dress.

He'd caught her a few months ago in a dress, and she'd looked so stunning, and so scared.

"I think you should show Slash a very good time," Dime said.

"I would love to take you all for a spin. Just line up, and I can take you better than any woman ever has in your life."

There was no temptation there. Nothing. He felt … nothing.

"I'm out of here."

"You're not sticking around to play?" Dime asked.

"You can play all by yourself. I don't want it." Getting up from his seat, he put the books back in the office, and left the club. He went straight to Devil and Lexie's house, which is where he normally found Natalie. Rarely did she leave, but he saw that the car the club had gotten for her was gone.

Knocking on the door, Lexie opened it, complete with her beaming smile. "Hey, Slash. You want Devil or Natalie?"

"Natalie, but I'll settle for a coffee."

She laughed. "Natalie's gone to the grocery store. She's taken Simon with her, so I wouldn't worry too much. That guy will talk her head off a mile a minute. He's taking a letter for Tabitha."

"I thought Devil had gotten the letter writing down to once a week?" Slash asked.

"He has."

Simon would write to Tabitha every single day, and when Devil finally saw how much that would cost in postage, he'd put a stop to it. Not only for his sanity, but also because it was entering serious stalker problems.

Slash was sure Tabitha and Simon often went a little overboard just to wind up their parents, or to freak them out.

There had been many times over the years that they'd played tricks on them. Slash often wondered what it would be like if Simon never got over his crush on Tabitha. The kid was convinced he was going to marry her.

Pushing those thoughts from his mind, he was pleased he didn't have to deal with any of that kind of shit.

Lexie poured him a coffee, and through the kitchen doors leading outside, he saw Devil with his kids, rolling around. It was a beautiful sunny day, not too hot or cold. Perfect family weather.

In that moment, Slash felt envious of the family Devil had. Lexie and the kids were his entire world, and everyone knew it. He loved his club, but his family came first, which none of them minded.

Lexie was one hell of a woman. Even when she didn't have to, she stripped to earn enough money to feed Simon. That was the club's biggest secret. Simon wasn't Lexie and Devil's son.

He'd slept with her sister, who'd then dumped Simon on Lexie, who in turn had been struggling to make ends meet. She lost her job, and ended up stripping in order to take care of a son who didn't belong to her.

In doing so, when Devil came to get his kid, he'd fallen hard for Lexie, and they'd stayed in Piston County. Lexie and Devil got married and had a great deal of sex.

Slash smiled at the love story with an erotic twist to it. It helped that Lexie was a woman who didn't take any shit from anyone.

She was a strong old lady, a fantastic mother, and a great friend.

"So, you, Butler, and Natalie."

He paused with the drink near his lips.

Lexie shrugged. "No one has any doubts about what is going on."

He took a sip of his drink, enjoying the taste. "Does she talk about me?"

"Natalie?" He nodded. "Natalie doesn't do a lot of talking, Slash. To be honest, she's probably one of the quietest women I've ever known. She's been through a lot from what Paris and Lola have told me. Considering they've been through hell—and they think she has, too—that's saying something."

Lola and Paris ended up being taken by one of the club's enemies. They'd had a few of them over the years. Their enemy had raped and beaten them before they could get to them. They'd lost a great deal over the years even as they'd found so much as well.

"Losing her parents and the ranch, it must have hurt her a lot."

"According to Paris, who went to school with her, Natalie never fit in. She was always drawing in her notebook, always wore boots for working. Rarely did she have the time for guys or even the girls. She didn't play, or care about getting attention. Since her father died and she sold the ranch, she's not been back yet."

Devil still had men maintain the ranch until they could figure out what to do with it. The club made a vow to her father to protect her. He'd fallen in love with her long before then.

"I want her, Lex. I love her more than anything in the world. I can't even begin to describe how much she fucking means to me." He paused. "What do I do?"

"You don't give up," Devil said, coming into the house.

Lexie turned toward him, smiling as he wrapped an arm around her waist.

Whenever Lexie was in a room, it was like his Prez couldn't keep his hands to himself.

"Do you really think Butler is interested in her?" Devil asked.

"He's not backing down. You saw him."

"I also saw the way he looked at our new cleaner, Mandy."

Slash had seen that as well, but Mandy had taken some time off to go and deal with family, and a new woman, a married woman with a spiteful bite and bitchy attitude, had taken her place. "Yeah, well since Mandy left, he's turned his attention back to Natalie, and I don't give a fuck what you say, he's going to stay on her case."

Devil shrugged. "I don't want a war brewing inside my club over a woman."

He didn't say anything. What could he say? Just because Butler eye fucked a different woman didn't mean shit.

****

Butler stood in the post office as Natalie arrived with Simon in tow. The kid wouldn't stop talking, even when they got to the counter. He watched as Natalie placed a small package to send to Lucius there. The club knew that the brother had gotten in touch with Natalie, and continued to text her.

No one had interfered. Even though Lucius was part of the club, he wasn't. He was a Chaos Bleeds, but he didn't follow any rules. The Nomads didn't have a Prez or any kind of leader. They lived by their own rules, but when they needed them, they came, it was as simple as that.

"Is Lucius all right?" he asked, stepping up behind Natalie, and placing a hand at her back.

"You scared me," she said.

"Natalie has a date," Simon said.

Butler glanced at Simon, who paid the clerk for his letter.

"Traitor," Natalie said.

"You have a date?"

"Yep," Simon said. "As soon as he found out that I wasn't her kid, he was all over her just like he was all over the fruit in the produce section."

"You accepted a date with a stranger?"

"A creepy stranger," Simon said.

She finished paying for her package and they all left the post office together. "Lucius is fine. He's … dealing. We don't really talk all that much. Sometimes he apologizes, which I think he does when he's really drunk because he can't spell when he can't see his cell. He just wanted a few items for his next stop."

"I don't care about him."

"You asked."

"Yeah, then Simon mentioned the creepy stranger."

"Yep, I did. Can we have ice cream? It's so hot right now, and I really could use an ice cream."

"Sure." They walked the few feet to the stand, and Natalie sighed. "He worked at the ranch. He's not a stranger. He's just a guy I know from a long time ago."

"So, he's an old dude who intends to take advantage of you."

"There's nothing to take advantage of. It's a date, and I'm hoping it will be fun." She tucked some hair behind her ear, and he saw her cheeks were flaming red.

"Why not ask me or Slash to take you out?" he asked.

"Look, with everything that is going on, I'm not … I don't want to be the cause of something."

"You think it's easier to date a stranger?"

"Yes, I do, because one day you and Slash will ask me to make a choice, and I don't want to do that. I don't want to be torn between the two of you. You're both my friends, were my friends. I…"

She didn't get to finish as the ice cream man opened up. She'd tried to keep them at arm's length. He got it. Natalie didn't want to hurt either of them, but going after a different guy, or trying to be with someone else, wouldn't cut it.

It was either him or Slash, no one else.

Chapter Three

"Do we even know this guy?" Devil asked.

Natalie took a bite of the steak, and felt so many different gazes on her. Chewing on her meat, she glanced up, catching Slash's eyes. Immediately she looked away as she saw the hurt within them. She didn't want to hurt anyone.

This thing going on between Slash and Butler scared her, and she wanted no part of it. She'd heard Paris talk about the Chaos Bleeds brotherhood as well as Lola, and that was something she refused to come between.

"He's a guy that used to work at the ranch."

"How come I don't know about him?" Devil wouldn't back down. "I know every single man working that ranch right this second, Natalie."

"He's one of the men that used to take the summer job. A few years older than me, and we'd hang out when he was around the ranch. He's a good guy." She saw the tight grip Slash had on his knife, and once again she was swamped by guilt.

You refuse to come between them.

"We're going out on Friday night to see a movie. It's nothing bad or anything." Why was she giving excuses or reasons? Devil wasn't her dad. *No, you don't have one of those anymore.* "I need some ketchup."

She got up from her seat and entered the kitchen, grabbing hold of the edge of the counter in an attempt to find whatever sanity she had left. This wasn't supposed to be hard or difficult.

Her life couldn't get any more complicated. It was going to be a simple date. That was all.

"You okay?" Slash asked.

She closed her eyes, counted to ten quickly, and spun around to see him staring at her. "Yeah, I'm fine." She reached into the fridge to grab the ketchup.

"Devil worries."

"He's not my dad."

"But your father asked him to take care of you. In all of the years I've known him, Devil doesn't do anything by half measures."

She'd come to see that. "I'm sorry."

"You don't need to apologize to me. He'll be an ass for some time. Probably put your date through the wringer." Slash shrugged.

Holding onto the ketchup, she couldn't bring herself to look away from Slash. She'd always found him to be a really handsome guy, and licking her lips, she was drawn to the firm line of his.

Can't happen.

"I wanted to apologize to you," he said.

"What about?"

"You wanted to sell the ranch for a long time. It was never your dream, and instead of listening to you, I ignored you, and I shouldn't have done that. I wanted to apologize for that."

"Oh, well, that is fine. Honestly."

"It's not. I knew you were unhappy, but losing something you've had all of your life, it's not easy. I should have understood that you've only ever done what your father wanted you to do."

"Thank you." She'd always felt a little guilty because he'd told her to wait, and she'd gone against him, selling it. Cutting herself free from the chains of her past. "Have you ever lost anything?"

"No."

"You never talk about your life before the club."

"I don't need to talk about my life before it, babe.

It's simple. I didn't have one before I joined Chaos Bleeds. No family, no hope, nothing."

She rubbed at her temple. "The Nomads never want to settle down."

"For the longest time we were Nomads. We all moved from place to place. Partying, causing shit." His smile had her pressing her thighs together, alarming her.

Slash was a sexy guy. If it wasn't his smile or the wicked glint in his eyes, it was his body. He was so hard, muscular. She'd caught him working out many times, and it had thrilled her each time to see it. The way his arms bulged as he lifted weights. One of the best sights in the world as far as she was concerned.

"Then you came here."

"Then we came here, and those of us that were finding it a little tiring decided to settle down." He spread his arms wide. "Piston County became our home, and the rest is history."

"You wanted to settle down?"

"I wanted to find a place to call home. I guess moving around has its place, but at the heart of everything, you want a place to call your own. This is our home."

Silence fell between them, and Natalie was becoming all too aware once again that she was a woman. She'd always been able to ignore the changes inside her because they didn't mean anything. Boys in high school never appealed, and her nights and weekends were often at the ranch hauling hay, cleaning out horse stalls, and doing all kinds of different jobs at the ranch.

Now that had changed.

She was living her dream, designing clothes, having more time for her art, and just enjoying her life. Still, something was missing.

Her stomach decided to growl, and Slash reached

out, taking her hand. The moment he touched her, she got a little zip of electricity from him. Every single time Slash touched her she got a buzz of something.

Entering the garden, she pulled her hand away because of all the curious eyes and took her seat. Once again, Devil began to ask questions about the man she'd agreed to go on a date with.

"Why haven't I seen him?"

"His name's John, you don't have to keep calling him date guy."

"Fine. Why have I never seen John if he's worked at the ranch?"

"I told you before I went for ketchup. He used to work during the summer. A couple of years ago he went away to college only he dropped out, and he's been traveling across Europe before getting back home."

"And now that he's home he wants to take you on a date."

"He's been gone long enough that he was surprised an MC club owned my father's ranch. I think he felt guilty for asking, seeing as my parents are both gone. He was a nice guy when I knew him, and I don't see what the fuss is about. Can we not talk about this right now, please?" she asked.

From the brief conversation with Slash, her emotions were all over the place, and she couldn't figure out why, and that scared her. She didn't want to feel anything for him. It was one of the reasons why she stopped watching him work out. It was easier than her body coming to life at the sight of him.

It never has for Butler.

He was safe, and she was sure the only reason he was near her was because she was safe to him. Not once when they'd been together had he tried anything. They were friends. Pushing those thoughts aside, she finished her meal. While the guys gathered around to have a smoke, and just generally talk, she helped Lexie do the dishes.

"I'm sorry about Devil giving you the third degree," she said.

"It's fine. Really, I'm getting used to it."

Lexie laughed. "Taking care of you is something serious to him, and he doesn't want you to be hurt."

She nodded, tucking some of her hair behind her ear. "I don't mind, not really. I know he means well."

Lexie moved up toward her, and cupped her face. "Are you happy to be going on this date?" Lexie was always very motherly. She was always there for everyone, taking care, being the old lady that Devil needed.

Natalie appreciated her strength. She was a fighter.

"It was a little unexpected because I've never been asked out before, and I didn't know what to say or do, but yeah, I'm happy."

"I know you don't want to come between the club."

"I won't, Lexie."

"Don't do something you'll regret, okay? I know it may seem easy to move on, but when the heart wants what it does, there's no getting away from that, and no one will blame you afterward."

"You're a wonderful woman," she said.

"You're not so bad yourself."

They finished doing the dishes, and after she helped Lexie get the kids ready for bed, she went to her room and began to sketch once again.

She was halfway through a second design when there was a knock at the door. "Come in."

Natalie looked up to see Devil entering her room.

He was still in his jeans and shirt from earlier. His leather cut was gone, though.

She sat up, and he shook his head. "You don't need to get up." He closed her door, and took a seat at one of her chairs, which he spun around so that his arms rested across the back.

"What's up?"

"Your father put his trust in me to take care of you. I've got a couple of girls I take care of. I'm not trying to make your life difficult. I'm taking care of you the way I imagine your father would any other girl that was entrusted to him."

This made her smile. "You're right. He wouldn't let them out of his sight without giving the third degree."

He pointed at her. "I know you're a grown woman, and can make your own decisions. I even respect that, but I'll still continue to take care of you even when you don't want it. I gave a man my word. My word means fucking law around here, and you can hate it, but I'm not going to change."

"So, I've got to learn to like it?"

"Yeah, you do, because I'm not changing."

She nodded. "Okay."

"You've got my numbers, and the club's. If at any point during your date you feel scared or threatened, you call me. Go to the toilet. Pretend to have the shits for all I care. You'll be collected and safe, Natalie."

"You're an amazing man, Devil."

"Thank you, I do try." He gave a little bow as he went toward the door.

"I won't break up your club," she said.

He turned back to her.

"Between Butler and Slash, I won't have them fighting."

Devil sighed. "I think you and I both know who

the real winner would be, honey."

He left her alone, and she sat back.

For the first time since moving in, she felt … whole.

****

"Could you be any more of a pain in the ass?" Snake asked.

"Fuck you," Slash said. He glanced at the clock and saw it was only a little after eight.

Natalie had already gone on her date. Devil had texted him to let him know she was gone, and it pissed him off.

"If it was going to bother you this much, why didn't you tail her?" Ripper asked, coming to take a seat at the bar. It was rare for Ripper to be without his woman, Judi, but they were all just finishing their work. Each of them took turns between the nightclub with the girls, the shop that Lexie managed, and several of their other projects. This week Ripper had the ranch, along with several brothers.

All of their income now came from legitimate businesses. There was a time they ran drugs, guns, all kinds of shit. They once ran anything that Ned Walker needed from them. Since settling down, and having one hell after another happen, none of them were interested in stepping on the wrong side of the wall.

In a way, it created a larger divide between the club and the Nomad Chapter. The brothers that stayed in Piston County could no longer have any vices like drink or drugs. Devil made a decision to get the entire club clean, especially as there had been a constant threat that could separate the club.

None of them were stupid enough to go against Devil. United they fight, divided they fall.

Slash had tasted drugs, but they'd never really

done anything for him. The high had been great, but afterward, coming down with a mighty thud wasn't what he wanted to experience again. Life was too fucking challenging without adding drugs to the mix.

"Shouldn't you be home?" he asked, looking at Ripper.

"My woman is spending time with Lexie. You know, her mother. So I'm waiting until she calls me to collect her."

Even though they all still had their bikes, several of the club brothers had to invest in a family car, Devil especially.

"You still didn't answer my question," Ripper said.

"I'm not tailing her."

"I thought you said you liked this woman," Snake said.

"You think if I like her I have to tail her? Watch her with her date?"

"It's what any sane man would do," Dick said, jumping up onto a stool and deciding to join in the conversation. "I wouldn't let Martha out of my sight, or for that matter, allow another club brother to think they can have her."

"Shut the fuck up," he said.

"Come on. We all know that Butler is just trying to create a shit storm. He's not really interested in Natalie. She's … safe to him," Dick said.

"Now a certain cleaner, that is a whole other thing all together." Spider joined in the conversation, and Slash wasn't finding it the least fun when they all seemed to be finding his annoyance … fun.

He knew that Butler wanted the cleaner, Mandy. At least he'd thought that, then of course, Mandy hadn't turned up for a few weeks because of personal problems, and now he had to deal with putting a spanner in the works with his own feelings for Natalie. He'd seen the way she looked at him in the kitchen the other day. The way her gaze had traveled down his body, and he'd even seen her pressing her thighs together. All telltale signs of a woman aroused, and instead of pulling her into his arms, he'd just left it.

Sucker!

"What I think needs to happen is you grow some balls," Dick said. "Once you got them, you'll be able to take Butler, and you'll both live happily ever after."

"Please, Slash can't take me," Butler said, finally arriving.

Slash stared at his friend and club brother. He'd die protecting every single man in the club, Butler included. Right now, he wanted to bury the man six feet under.

"Now that Butler is here, the real fun can begin."

"Want to play a game?" Butler asked, holding up his pool cue.

Slash grabbed one and began to prepare the tip as Butler lined up the balls on the table.

"You can break," Butler said.

Leaning forward, he aligned the shot and took it.

There was a round of cheers.

"So tell me, Butler," Dick said. "Heard from Mandy yet?"

The moment Dick asked his question, the aim that Butler had went off to the side, and he missed his shot. "Mandy who?"

"Nice try, hotshot. You had that in the bag until he mentioned her name." Slash leaned forward, and took aim.

"I took Natalie out for ice cream."

He jerked, and the ball hit the side of the table,

bouncing several of the balls.

Glaring at the smirk on Butler's face, Slash stepped away. Devil had told them both he didn't want any fucking fights between them. If either of them came to blows, and something was damaged, Devil would demand they pay for everything.

He didn't mind paying the money, it was the fucking cleanup, and punishment that Devil would make them both do. Being part of the club put Devil in charge, and he didn't get his name lightly.

No one danced with the Devil or tested him without coming out burned, or even worse. "She dropped something on the floor and bent forward. The shirts she wears cover those curves, but damn, if they don't half gape. Her tits looked so fucking precious."

Slash squeezed the pool cue, as he wanted to shove the stick right up Butler's ass.

"Mandy's not half bad either. When she bends over, her ass sticks up in the air, and I swear it's begging to be slapped," Dime said, joining the conversation. "I've watched her clean a couple of times, and wondered just how good she'd feel wrapped around my cock. She's got a fire inside her, you know. The kind that heads to the bedroom where you burn up the sheets."

Butler charged toward Dime, but this time Slash stepped in.

"Fucking don't," Slash said.

"What the fuck are you saying?" Butler got up into his face.

"If this is what another brother does to you simply *talking* about Mandy, giving you little suggestions of exactly what he'd like to do to her, then why the fuck are you trying to take what belongs to me?" Slash stepped up close to Butler.

"What's the matter, Slash, afraid of a little

competition?"

"No, I'm not. Unlike you, I fucking care about Natalie. You know what, let's cut this bullshit right now. I don't just care about her, I fucking love her, and you're playing with her feelings, you piece of shit. The moment Mandy comes back and looks your way, or she's not a fucking cleaner anymore, you'll drop Natalie like she's got a fucking disease to chase after someone else." He got right up in Butler's face. "That's what I don't like. I'm not afraid of you, Butler. Never have been, never will be. You hurt the woman I love. You break her heart if she chooses you, then you better run, cause brother or not, there'll be a special plot with your name on it six feet fucking under, even if I lose my patch to kill you."

Silence rang through the club.

Not only would taking Butler out take Slash's patch, there would also be a vote on what to do with him. Let him go as a civilian, marking him so everyone knew he was a traitor, or killing him.

It was a serious offense to kill one of their own, unless sufficient reason was given.

Snake's cell phone rang, cutting through the tension. Slash didn't back down, and neither did Butler.

His threat had surprised Butler though.

"Shit, are you sure?" Snake asked. "Fuck, we'll get there right away."

Snake closed his cell phone.

"That was Jessica. Natalie and her date have just been brought in. Natalie's in a coma right now. They've both been beaten up pretty badly."

Slash was gone. Climbing onto his bike outside of the clubhouse, he gunned the engine and drove toward the hospital. On the way there, he hated himself for letting her go alone, for not being there.

All kinds of scenarios entered his head. Natalie in

a coma. Her dying.

No, this couldn't be happening.

He broke every single speed limit to get to the hospital. Jessica was waiting for him as he climbed off his bike.

"How is she?"

"She's stable right now, but in critical condition."

Jessica didn't try to stop him as he entered the hospital, and showed him where Natalie was.

Slash paused outside Natalie's door and stared at the woman who lay hooked up to machines.

"Not all the swelling has come down, or the bruises. She has several broken ribs, and took several blows to the—"

"Jessica, tell Devil, not me. I can't … not right now." He entered Natalie's room and took a seat.

He'd not been there, and someone had hurt her.

He hadn't fucking been there!

His anger began to build as he stared at his woman. She shouldn't have been on a date with anyone else.

Natalie belonged to him, and he was done playing with this bullshit.

****

Devil had seen Natalie. He hadn't gone into the room, and he didn't disturb Slash either. The club was in the main reception, including the old ladies. They were all worried about Natalie. Even though the young woman didn't talk all that much, or involve herself, she was part of them.

Lexie cared about her, and often talked about her to him, and her father had begged him to keep an eye on her.

Right now, he needed fucking answers, and he stared at the fucker who had just woken up.

Butler was in the room, along with Snake. Jessica was keeping an eye outside. The man before him was beaten up pretty badly, but he wasn't in a coma with swelling on the brain, or the risk that he might not wake up.

If Natalie died, he fucking failed. If that happened … he couldn't bring himself to think of what to do if that happened. Whenever he gave his word, he kept it. Natalie dying, his word wouldn't be kept, and he couldn't have that.

"How is she?" John asked, his voice rough and hoarse.

"She's in a coma," Devil said. "Doctors don't know if she'll wake up, or if that's how she's going to be for the rest of her life." Jessica had told them before seeing her that if she didn't wake up or show any sign of brain activity, then they'd ask him to turn off her machines. Right now, it hadn't come to that, but he'd demanded Jessica give him the worst-case scenario.

He was paying for her treatment, and he would decide if she died or not.

It hadn't come to that.

"I don't know you, and right now, I don't like you. You see, Natalie doesn't belong to you. She never had, but she wanted to go on this date, and being the nice guy that I am, I let her. But here is my problem, John, you've not brought her back in one piece. That's all I asked." Devil stepped forward. "I'm not a very nice person when I don't get what I want."

"I didn't hurt her. We were watching a movie. We decided to go to one of those, erm, those movie places where you sit in the car?"

"A drive-in. I know what one is."

"We were minding our own business, just watching an old black and white film, and some guys came around. They started asking for money and stuff. I told them to fuck off, and they pushed Natalie to the ground and started kicking her. I paid them everything I had, and tried to get them to stop, but I couldn't." John looked ready to burst into tears.

"They started on you."

"Yeah, they did."

"Did they rape her?" Snake asked.

Devil jerked as he'd not even considered that, his anger fueling him.

"No. Before I passed out, I know someone came to us. They put a stop to it. I'm sorry."

He stepped up close and stared at the broken man. "You stay away from Natalie. She's not yours, but until I find the men responsible for this, you're now club property, and you will have a brother at your side until you identify them."

John nodded.

Leaving the room, Devil didn't stop as he made his way out for some fresh air. He had to take some deep breaths, because murdering John right now wouldn't answer his questions.

Lexie came out to him. She rubbed his back, and her touch alone was enough to calm the beast raging inside.

"You okay, baby?" she asked.

"No, I'm not." He pulled her into his arms, kissing her head and breathing her in. Her scent allowed him to relax.

"Do I need to start worrying?"

"I'm not going to start killing people in the town."

"That's not what I mean."

"It's not another threat."

"You're sure."

He nodded. "Yeah. This is just a group of kids that don't even realize they messed with the wrong girl."

"Do you think she'll pull through?"

"I don't know, baby. I don't know."

"How's Slash?"

"Just watching her. I'm not going to pull him out. Right now, Slash is where he needs to be."

There was no way he'd pull Slash away from Natalie's side. He needed him watching her, taking care of her. Making sure she was okay.

"Don't feel guilty about this."

"You're always worrying about me."

"I'll worry about you for the rest of my life, Devil." She kissed his lips. "That's the point of marrying the love of your life."

He held her close.

He would find the people responsible and they better hope they were kids, because otherwise, they were about to meet their maker.

Chapter Four

Natalie hadn't woken up yet, and Slash continued to stare at her. He ignored the nurses and doctors who came in to take care of her. Lexie came in with Simon in tow, to drop him off some food, and a coffee.

Simon took the spare seat. "She'll be okay," he said.

"We know, honey." Lexie rubbed his hair, and Simon pulled out of her grip and pushed his hair in a different direction.

Slash smiled.

"You okay?" Lexie asked.

"I will be. She's stable, and there's no change. She has brain activity, so the doctors think her body is just trying to repair itself, and I shouldn't worry."

"You wouldn't be you unless you worried," Lexie said. "She'll pull through."

He watched as Simon grabbed Natalie's hand.

"Come on, son, we've got to go."

"But it's a Saturday. I can stay here with her."

"No, let's leave Slash alone with his woman."

"Is she yours?" Simon asked. "You're going to claim her for like real now, not pretend?"

Slash smiled. "She was always mine, Simon. She just didn't know it yet."

"She wants a man who knows how to be the handsome prince, and who can protect her."

He frowned. "What?"

"I heard her say it to Elizabeth. They were talking after my sister read some weird book about a sparkling vampire. How she wanted a boyfriend to be nice and everything, and Natalie said that having a good guy is great, and you want a good guy, but you also need to have a guy who knows what he wants, and is not afraid to get it. I thought you should know." Simon waved goodbye and Lexie shrugged.

Sitting forward, he reached out and moved some of her hair off her face. "You want a biker, baby?" he asked. He could live with that. Being a gentleman and a bad boy.

He sat there for several more minutes until he heard a throat clearing.

Butler stood inside the door. He held a bouquet of flowers.

"I'm not here to cause problems."

"Then why are you here?" Slash asked.

"Can we have a truce?"

"Can you stop pretending that you want her? She's not yours, Butler, she never has been."

"I like her."

"I love her."

Butler sighed. "Look, I enjoy being around her, okay. You're always too gentle with her, and you never really listened."

"I listened."

"Then why did you make her feel guilty for wanting to sell the ranch?"

He had nothing else to say, and gritted his teeth. He didn't mean to make her feel guilty. When she mentioned it, he thought it was the grief talking, and he didn't want her to do something that would hurt her later on.

The club had the ranch, and she was taken care of. He'd seen her happier than ever before. Making her keep the ranch was a bad idea.

"Why are you here?" Slash asked.

"Believe it or not, I do like her." Butler held his hands up. "I don't love her, and I'm not going to even pretend that I do. I care about her, and she's a nice woman, and I'm sorry."

"What?"

"I'm sorry, okay. I thought … I thought I wanted her, but last night, yeah, it's not going to happen, and I don't want to hurt her, but she doesn't inspire me like that. I don't think about her in that kind of way." Butler placed the flowers on the counter. "You shouldn't keep her at arm's length though. I've seen some of her more erotic sketches that she's done. I stole her book, and looked at them. Natalie wants passion in her life, she just doesn't know how to get it."

"When she wakes up, I'm not backing down."

"You shouldn't."

Butler left them alone, and Slash stared at his woman. The bruising had come out now, and one of her eyes was swollen shut. He didn't even need to have her eyes open to see that.

"I'm not going to let you out of my sight again." He grabbed her hand, resting his head against her fingers, and he actually prayed for her to wake up.

Time passed, and the sounds of the hospital seemed to fade as he just allowed himself to be with Natalie.

If she didn't make it, he didn't know what he'd do. He couldn't think straight, nor did he want to.

"You can't die," he said.

There was a knock on the door, and he looked up and frowned. Lucius, from the Nomad Chapter, who had kissed her, stood in the doorway. He held an art book and pens in his hands.

"What are you doing here?" Slash asked.

"Natalie told me she had a date. When I didn't hear anything, I called Devil. He told me what happened."

He was aware that Natalie and Lucius had been texting. Before Roxy died, Natalie had gotten close to the other woman, and he knew she'd asked her to keep in touch with Lucius, to make sure he wasn't alone.

They were friends.

There had never been any feelings between the two, even though Lucius had kissed her, but he'd done that to start a fight.

"That doesn't explain what you're doing here."

"Making sure she's okay." Lucius glanced down at his gifts. "Roxy..." His voice broke, and he cleared it. "Roxy really liked her."

"Does Devil know you're here?"

"Knowing Devil, he does. Have I gone to see him? No."

"Why not?"

"There's no point."

"Have you ever thought about settling down in one place?" Slash asked.

"Nope. I'm not that kind of guy. I'll never settle down in one place, and I have no intention of starting it now." Lucius placed his gifts on the small table where everyone seemed to want to place their stuff. "When she wakes up, tell her thanks."

Lucius didn't wait around, and within seconds he was gone.

Slash sat back, and rubbed at his eyes. He understood that Lucius was in pain. Losing someone close to you would have that effect on a person, and once again, his attention was brought right back to the woman on the hospital bed.

He wouldn't survive losing her. There was no doubt about it in his mind. She was everything to him, and when she got out of this hospital bed, he was done playing around. Butler could go and fuck himself. He was done playing nice.

Natalie belonged to him, and it was about time she realized it.

****

"There's still no change?" Lexie asked. She held her empty cup. Hot chocolate always had a way of soothing her problems, but not right now. Natalie being in a coma was really upsetting. They'd all gotten attached to the little designer. She was their family, even if she didn't realize it herself.

"No, still no fucking change," Devil said. He removed his leather jacket and placed it on the back of the sofa.

"Did you go to the Sheriff?"

"Yep, and it would appear there have been several break-ins and beatings going up and down this town, and across several of them."

"You don't think this is a hit out on the club?" Lexie asked.

"Nope. Talking with the good old Sheriff, it would seem there's a group of men trying to make a name for themselves. They can't be sure if it's youths or older. Either way, I catch up to them, and they're going to be in for some really harsh fucking reality."

She was used to her husband talking about killing people. She knew he did it, too. Even though he took lives, she still loved him. Rarely did Devil take the lives of the innocent. She smiled, thinking about his name and how apt it was. He was judge, juror, and executioner. Anything that touched his family or the club had to go through him.

"What's that smile on your lips?" he asked, moving toward the sofa.

He wrapped his arms around her shoulders and pulled her close. "I'm thinking about Natalie." It wasn't a total lie.

"She's got to pull through," Devil said.

"If she doesn't?"

"We'll have another brother go off the rails. Speaking of, Lucius made it into town today. He dropped some gifts off for Natalie and left."

"So he's alive."

"Yeah, he's alive. Not looking good, according to Slash. At least he didn't try and get himself killed this time." He stroked her arm and she closed her eyes.

"You always take care of everything."

"It's what a Prez does. I should have known I'd end up a dad sooner or later. I'm one to a bunch of boys refusing to grow up."

She chuckled. "The club adores you, and you love it. You love being the big old daddy." She gave a little squeal as he moved her so that she was straddling his lap.

"I know what I like to be a whole lot more than just a daddy."

"Oh, yeah, and what's that?"

"Balls deep inside you."

****

Dear Tabitha,

It's me again, and I miss you. I hope you get these letters and your dad isn't throwing them in the trash. Hey, Tiny and Eva, if you are. So, shit has hit the fan again. Natalie got beat up, and I saw her. She looks really, really bad. Her face is all bruised up as if she's been punched, and the doctors are all worried. So is my dad. We all like her. She doesn't talk all that much, Natalie. She listens, draws, and cooks. That's about it. Slash loves her completely, you know. Totally, one hundred percent loves her.

Not a lot is happening right now. I'm going to

school, and I hate history. It's so boring learning about the past. What is the point of it? We know what's already happened. Move on already. I want to know what is happening today, and they don't talk about any of the MC either. MC is totally in my blood, and you should know. It's in yours.

There are times I hate writing. I always have so many questions, and I have to wait for the answers, or what you have to say. I don't know when I'll get to send this letter. I love writing because it gives me something to do. See, I'm a total weirdo, but if you tell anyone I said that I'll deny it.

So here are my questions.
Have you missed me?
Did you have a fun vacation in Vegas?
What's your favorite topic in school?
Do you like going to school?
What's happening over there?
Do you have any questions for me?
Short and sweet.
Take care, Tabby.
Love, your Simon.

****

"You stink," Jessica said, moving to open a window.

It had been five days since Natalie was brought in, and Slash didn't want to leave her side or miss a moment with her. He didn't give a shit how he smelled or what the fuck was going on in the world. Natalie hadn't gotten worse, nor had she gotten better. The bruising had all come out, and at least with her asleep, she wasn't in any kind of pain. They gave her some morphine, and it was starting to really get to Slash that she wasn't waking up.

"Then leave."

"What is wrong with taking five minutes to have a bath or even a shower? Do you even deodorize?"

"I'm not leaving Natalie."

"I'll be here. I won't move from this spot."

"If you get called away."

"I can phone someone from the club," Jessica said.

"Not happening. I'm not going to risk it."

"What exactly are you risking?"

"I want to be here when she wakes up, Jessica. If I stink, I don't care, so long as she sees that she's not alone. I'm not going to risk her being hurt because no one turned up. It's just … it's not happening."

"Okay," she said. She held her hands up. "I was just thinking she'd wake up a lot sooner if the smell wasn't so bad."

Sitting back, Slash glared at her. "Why does Snake put up with you?"

"Because I'm awesome, and he's very much aware of that."

"I call bullshit."

She burst out laughing. "You would because you don't understand awesome." She stopped by the door, arms folded, looking so happy with herself. "I never thought I'd see the day Slash would fall for a woman."

"What's that supposed to mean?"

"Come on, Slash, you've been one of the biggest man-whores I've ever known. Whenever there was free pussy, you were all over that. Now look at you. You'd rather sit stinking than leave your woman." Jessica's gaze landed on the bed, and her face froze. "And doesn't your woman have the prettiest eyes you've ever seen."

He looked at Natalie, and he saw at least one eye was open. She seemed confused at first, and as the seconds passed, she began to panic, realizing she'd been hooked up to several machines.

"It's okay," he said. There was a tube in her mouth to assist with her breathing, and Jessica was there as she was a nurse at the hospital, helping to take it out. She clicked a button, and it wasn't long before several nurses and doctors were in the room. Slash didn't leave, and watched as Natalie was brought up to speed on everything that had happened.

She was given some water to help rehydrate her, and he stood back, so fucking happy that she was alive. There was always that risk, he knew, of her falling under and never coming back.

Finally, as the doctors filed out, Jessica let him know that she'd call Devil and give him the heads up. The hospital would alert the Sheriff, and he'd be there in no time with his questions.

"Slash," Natalie said.

She tried to sit up, and he quickly moved to her side, and helped her. "Easy."

"I feel like I've been run over by a bus, and it backed up, going over me again." He cupped her cheek, and she smiled. "You stayed with me?"

"Do you really think there would be anywhere else I'd want to go?"

"I don't know."

Her voice was scratchy, and he held the drink in front of her, getting her to sip through the straw. She stopped and leaned back.

"Do you remember anything?" he asked.

"I was with John, and then we were surrounded by a bunch of men, and they were goading each other. They started to hit John, and I tried to stop them, and they began to hit me. Nothing … nothing happened, did it?"

"You weren't raped." He took hold of her hand

and pressed a kiss to it.

"I think I passed out from the pain."

"Someone called for help, and it stopped them."

"I've been such a pain in the ass," she said.

"Don't even for a second think that we're upset about being here for you. You're part of us, Natalie. We love you, and we'll take care of you. Whoever did this to you better pray the cops find them first."

"You shouldn't be saying stuff like that," she said. "What if people hear you?"

"I don't give a fuck who hears me. I get my hands on them, they're going to wish they'd never laid eyes on you."

She glanced around the room. "There are so many flowers."

"All for you. Lucius stopped by. He said thank you for everything." He pointed to the gifts. "He brought you those."

"Will you call him? Tell him I'm alive and awake."

"Yes, I'll do that."

She leaned in a little closer. "Could you also take a shower? I don't mean to be offensive, but you do stink a bit."

"Were you listening to Jessica tell me what to do?"

"Was she telling you to take a shower?"

"Yes."

"Then you should thank her. I heard what she was telling you."

Slash chuckled, leaning in close and kissing her head. "Your wish is my command." He stroked her cheek, and she wrinkled her nose. "I'm going. I'm going. It's good to have you back."

****

Even though she was in agony, Natalie was happy. She'd spoken to the Sheriff, who had already gotten a statement from John. He wasn't in the hospital anymore, but from what she'd been told, he was with the club. She didn't even want to think why the club was holding John. What happened wasn't his fault.

Slash returned from taking a shower, and the musty smell had disappeared from the room. He looked a million times better, and he was also smiling. She loved his smile. It brightened his entire face, and made her melt, seeing him.

He sat in his chair, and when the food came around, the nurses brought them extra so he could have some.

Natalie was shocked by the sudden flash of jealousy that rushed through her as the nurses flirted with him. She'd never been jealous before, not that she could ever remember, and she didn't want him looking to them for anything.

She took a bite of the mashed potatoes, and wrinkled her nose. They weren't that good. Slash dug in, taking a healthy portion.

"You haven't asked about Butler," he said.

She paused with the fork poised against her lips. "What?"

"I thought you'd ask about him?"

"Why?"

"You know, him having feelings for you and all."

And once again she felt uncomfortable.

"We all know that Butler doesn't have true feelings for Natalie. He cares about you, sweetie, but that's about it. You know that."

"Hey, Devil," she said, smiling.

He stood in the doorway of her hospital room. "You gave us a fright."

"I'm sorry."

"You've got nothing to be sorry about. You really do need to stop apologizing because you really, really don't need to." Devil entered the room. "Lexie wanted to come, and she said as soon as you're well enough, girl's night. She's already picked the movie and invited Judi. I get to take care of the kids while you do." He sat down in the spare seat.

"I miss her, too."

Devil eased back and stared at her. "Did you know any of them?"

"No. They were just … it was like they wanted a fight. John was there, and he tried to handle them. He gave them what money he had, and they just started hitting him. They were in a group. I didn't count them or anything."

"Then they started to hit you?"

"Yes."

Devil shook his head. "What were they wearing?"

"Hoodies. They looked like kids, but they could have been college age, I'm not sure. I didn't even see their faces. They just kept shouting to hit and hit harder. To make it hurt." She paused, recalling the shouts along with the screams.

Slash caught her hand and gave it a squeeze.

"Until we find the ones responsible, you'll have a guard at your side. One of the brothers will be with you, and I don't want arguments. All of the old ladies are getting them."

"You think this has to do with the club?" Slash asked.

"Nope. I think this is a bunch of kids who think they're all big and tough. I want to find them, and with a man with each of the women, I've got a bigger chance. All of my contacts are on the lookout as well. I've also got Lola going through security footage, and different cameras. She's trying to find the one near your car that night. A lot of cameras are around Piston County."

He leaned across the bed and pressed a kiss to her forehead. It reminded her of what her father would often do when she wasn't well. "Take care."

She watched him leave and turned toward Slash. "Is Butler here?"

"What?"

"Is he? Is he sitting beside you right now, waiting to see if I'm okay?" she asked.

"No."

"Then don't bring him up. Don't keep mentioning him."

From the moment the men had started to hurt John and then herself, she'd been thinking of Slash. Hoping he'd been close, but knowing it was hopeless to think that he was. She stared at him as he finished off his yogurt.

Hospital food was disgusting, and yet he didn't complain.

Whenever she was around Slash, he always made her feel so many different things. Butler, he was her friend, and right now, she felt like she'd been opened up and exposed. She'd been able to keep them at arm's length, but now she didn't know what to do. Slash was here, and she hadn't been disappointed to find him waiting.

"What are you thinking?" he asked.

"A woman can never tell her secrets."

He laughed. "You can tell me your secrets any time."

"I don't think I should have gone on that date."

"I wish you hadn't, but there's nothing you can do about that now."

"I never wanted to hurt you," she said. "I don't want to come between club brothers."

He touched her hand once again.

The moment he touched her skin, she felt like she was on fire for all the right reasons. She loved his touch and couldn't get enough of it.

"You won't." They stared at each other for the longest time, neither of them saying anything more. "Eat your food. You'll need your strength."

Chapter Five

It was time for her to go home three days after waking up, and Natalie had finally looked in the mirror and winced. She looked a mess, and couldn't believe that not only had Slash been so attentive, he'd not even seemed to notice that her face was messed up.

"I'm ugly," she said.

"You could never be ugly. Now stop being a big baby and put a beautiful smile on that face. No one wants to see a miserable bitch," Slash said.

He picked up her bags, and took her hand, pulling her against him. She didn't fight him, wrapping her arms around his waist and staring up into his eyes.

She didn't deserve this man. Even after all this time, he was there, at the hospital with her. He was the first man to offer to take her home, and the only one she trusted right now.

"The bruises will fade in time. They're already fading, and it won't be long before I can see both of those beautiful eyes that you try to keep hidden."

She chuckled. "I don't try to keep them hidden."

"You've always got your head in a book, or sketching. I rarely get to see those eyes."

She'd change that.

"Come on, let's take you home." She kept hold of his hand as they made their way out of the hospital. No one stopped them. According to one of the nurses, the club had taken care of all of her medical bills, so she didn't have to worry about a thing.

Even though she ached all over, she was glad to be going home. Slash put her bag in the back, and she lowered herself into the car, trying not to jolt or shock anything with any kind of force.

He climbed behind the wheel and started up the car.

"I don't suppose we can take it easy heading home? I don't think I'm going to be such a great passenger," she said.

"Ah, no problem at all, babe," he said.

They pulled out of the hospital, and there was that customary speed bump. He went over it so slowly that several cars beeped at him. She closed her eyes, but Slash wouldn't be budged as he moved over it. There was no pain at all, and she looked toward him. "Thank you."

"All you've got to do is ask and you shall receive. Here. You'll be wanting this." He handed her cell phone over to her.

Opening it up, she saw several missed calls and messages from Lucius.

Dialing his number, she waited.

"It's about time you called me," Lucius said.

"Thank you for the gifts. They were really sweet."

"It's the least I could do. Do they have any idea yet who did that to you?" he asked.

"Nope. No idea."

"Do you need me to come back?"

She looked toward Slash. "No, I'm okay here. Unless you're ready to come back."

"I'm not coming back to Piston County, Natalie."

"You're not. What about Roxy?"

"I can't come back."

She nodded. "I get it."

"I'm really pleased you're well, sweetheart. You're too sweet to be in any kind of pain."

She chuckled. "I don't know about sweet."

"I tell you what, I know who I've got my money

on winning your hand, and it's the man right beside you. Slash deserves you. He loves you, honey. I saw it when I came to visit. Butler's nowhere to be seen. He doesn't deserve you. Any guy that really wants you is there for you, no matter what."

She gritted her teeth, refusing to cry right now. "Thank you."

"Don't thank me. Just think about it. Also, start carrying around a gun. It's time you learned how to shoot."

"I already know."

"You do?"

"My dad made sure I knew how to shoot a shotgun, Lucius. I can take care of myself."

"Well, now, you better tell Slash to keep you because otherwise screw them, you're mine."

This time, she giggled. "Goodbye, Lucius."

"Goodbye."

She hung up the phone.

"Do I need to worry about you shooting my ass or something?" Slash asked.

"Nah. Lucius said it was time for me to learn to shoot, but I already know how. I used to have to use Daddy's shotgun often. He used it to go out into the fields to scare the birds away from the feed. It never really worked, and I could never shoot them either." She shrugged. "I don't like hurting anything."

"Did he say anything else?" he asked.

She rested her head in her hand and glanced over at him. "That I should pick you."

Once again Slash smiled. "See, I knew there was a reason why I liked him."

"He also said that you're on a countdown if you don't win me yourself because he'll take me. I think he's got a thing for women who can shoot guns."

"Well, damn, that is hot. You do know how to shoot?"

"Yes, I do."

Slash glanced over at her. "I think I'm safe from him."

"Yeah, he's not coming back to Piston County."

"Do you ever think of leaving?"

"Sometimes. My memories here are not bad. It's home, you know. My dad would want me to be taken care of."

"The club will always take care of you, Natalie. Don't ever doubt that."

"I won't. I love the club as well."

They pulled into the main drive of Lexie and Devil's house. She'd already caught sight of all the bikes and some of the cars.

"I think it's safe to say this is the worst-kept surprise welcome home party," he said. "Are you ready to go inside or would you like me to drive around a little more?"

She wanted him to drive around a little more, but she didn't want to be rude. "Maybe take me driving a little later."

"You're on."

He climbed out of the car and was by her side, helping her as she struggled not to wince or moan.

"I really do need to get a handle on this. I don't want to get used to having someone help me get out of a car."

"I'll always be here to help you." She put her arm through his, and maybe put a little too much weight on his arm as they made their way inside.

A full round of cheers went up, and she smiled as the club welcomed her home.

Devil, Lexie, and all the kids were there. Judi and

Ripper, along with their two. Everywhere that she looked were Chaos Bleeds.

"We're happy to have you home," Lexie said, rushing toward her and pulling her in for a hug.

It was so unexpected the pain hit her quickly, and she winced.

"Shit, I'm so sorry. I didn't … ugh, this is going to be hard."

"Mom needs to put some money in the jar," Simon said.

Lexie rolled her eyes, but left to go and put some money in the curse jar. Natalie laughed, and each person hugged her in a way that tried not to jar her body or hurt her in any way, which wasn't easy. In fact, it was hard for them to do, but she dealt with it.

Gritting her teeth through most of it.

With Slash by her side, she could handle it.

He gave her strength.

Devil had already lit the grill, and food was cooking. She was told to just relax, and that she didn't have to worry about taking care of the kids or anything.

Slash left her in the garden, and she watched as men and women talked. The kids were splashing around with Ripper and Judi in the pool, and everyone was just being one big happy family.

"Hey," Butler said.

He wrapped an arm around her shoulders and pulled her close. He did it in such a way that she wasn't in any kind of pain.

"Hey." There were no feelings. She cared about Butler. He was a friend, but those feelings weren't there. "How have you been?"

"Taking care of business. I've spent a great deal of time with Lola. We've been going through the footage, trying to find anything that could identify the men that attacked."

She nodded.

"So, I was wondering if you'd be willing to go out for a ride with me later," Butler said.

Natalie stared at him, and shook her head. "No."

"No?"

It was the first time she'd ever refused him, or a chance to go out for a ride. She loved the fresh air and getting away from life, but this wasn't going to happen. Not between them.

"You and I both know that you don't want me, Butler. We're not meant to be. There's someone else you want and it isn't me."

She wasn't good with emotions, or at least speaking them. Working on a ranch surrounded by men, she'd only seen and heard how blunt they could be. She didn't want to hurt anyone's feelings, but she also didn't see a reason to pretend that something was okay when it really wasn't.

Butler laughed. "Okay."

"We're friends. That's all we'll ever be. This is not about being a sore loser or anything."

"Slash was there?" he asked.

"It's not just that. Slash was always there, Butler. You weren't. You just allowed me to speak my mind without giving any input. I see that now. Slash, he wanted what's best for me, and that's okay. I don't mind."

When Slash had started coming around to the ranch, she'd often hide because she hated blushing. He was the first guy to make her blush and feel so damn young. It was only when her father didn't give her much of a choice and she hung out with him, that her crush really began to form. Of course, that changed after her father died, but she was grieving, so her feelings for

Slash didn't seem all that important. She'd never known such pain and guilt. The ranch was her father's dream.

She wanted to design.

Throughout all of it, Slash had been there, and now she realized he'd not been trying to manipulate her at all.

He'd been trying to help her so she didn't make a decision she'd regret.

Slash walked toward her, holding a cup. "I thought you were thirsty."

"I am." She took the drink from him.

Going on a date, and getting beat up, had kickstarted her feelings, her own desires once again.

Either that, or she needed to see a doctor, which she doubted.

****

Slash didn't leave her side other than to get her drinks and food. She spent most of it watching everyone, and he noticed that she did that often. Even before her attack, at a party in the clubhouse, she simply stood or sat watching everyone, rarely joining in.

It had taken him some time to figure out that she didn't have the first clue how to join in. If she didn't wince every couple of minutes, he'd have taken her to the pool, or danced with her. He stood by her side, and talked with everyone that came their way.

When she seemed to withdraw into herself, he put his arm around her back and kept her close, offering her the comfort of his own body.

After several hours passed, people began to leave, and he took Natalie to Devil, letting him know he was taking her for a ride.

"You sure you want to go for a ride?" Devil asked, which pissed him off, but one thing he would always say about his Prez, he was protective.

They'd not gotten to where they were today without him.

"I want to go with him."

"Okay. Let us know if you're going to be back late," Devil said.

"Did you get the sense that he was treating you like a daughter?" Slash asked, opening her car door for her.

"He always does. It's how he'd want someone to take care of his little girl. I wouldn't take it personally. He's just taking care." She reached for the seat belt and winced. "I hate this. I hate feeling like each movement is on fire."

He leaned forward, and buckled her seatbelt. "You'll get better. You're just going to have to learn to take help when it's offered."

She smiled. "And you'll be the one doing the offering?"

"Hell, yeah. Of course." He winked at her and she rolled her eyes, which made him laugh. Climbing behind the wheel, he pulled away from the house and started toward town. He wanted to take her to his place.

He'd purchased a rundown house on the outskirts of town in a small neighborhood. The yard was big, and when he first saw it, he'd wanted to fill it with kids, lots of them.

"I told Butler that I didn't have any feelings for him other than being friends."

He gripped the steering wheel even tighter. When he'd been getting them drinks, he'd caught sight of Butler talking to her. He'd had to stay still for a few minutes, and remind himself that it was a family gathering for Natalie, and Devil didn't want him murdering a club brother in his garden.

"And?"

"We both know that I'm not the one Butler wants. We're friends, and I don't make him want to be a better man. I'm safe territory when it comes to him."

"You don't mind that?"

"Of course not. Butler was always safe as well."

"You think only relationships work where the man wants to be better for the woman?" he asked.

"No. I just think that relationships are always better when both people want to try as hard as possible for the ones they love. Don't you think that's how it works?"

He thought about it, and in a way, yes. He wanted to be better for Natalie.

"Yeah, I do."

She laughed. "You don't have to keep agreeing with me."

"I'm not. Say something I don't agree with, I'll even fight you for it."

He loved hearing her laugh. It had been too long since she'd been relaxed enough in his company to let go, and he wasn't going to mess it up now.

"I've missed this," she said.

"What?"

"Being with you. Us talking."

"My feelings for you haven't changed."

"I know, but now it doesn't feel like I'm going to come between two brothers. I'm not like that. I don't want you or Butler fighting, and besides, he's not in love with me. He cares about me, and that's about it." She shrugged. "And no, before you even think to ask, I don't care that he's not in love with me."

He wasn't going to argue with that. Butler was out of the running, and he'd have gladly ended the fucker's life, but he was also a club brother. Dick had survived this long, and he was a total asshole. Butler wasn't anything like him. He'd been competition, and now he wasn't.

Pulling up into the long drive, he parked the car and stared up at his home. It needed a lot of work.

"You bought this?"

"It was going at auction. I didn't pay all that much. No one else wanted it," he said.

"Erm, Slash, it's falling down."

"I've had several building contractors out. It's structurally sound. It just hasn't been taken care of for a long time, so it has fallen into disrepair. Nothing a bit of love and a lot of work won't fix. I'm part of a club, and they'll help."

He climbed out of the car and went to her side, opening the door and easing her out.

The land was big, and every time he was here, he imagined lighting up the grill, kids running around. The club staying, maybe pitching some tents so they could enjoy a drink.

Natalie linked her arm with his, and they made their way inside the home. He'd already had several locks installed.

"The outside needs some serious paintwork, and several of the boards are missing."

"I don't know if I've told you this before, but I'm pretty good with my hands."

"Nope, I don't think you've ever said anything," she said, laughing.

Opening the door, he reached in, flicking on the light. There were walls missing, but the electricity was sound. He'd already had all the relevant people out to check everything over. He didn't want to show Natalie around a place that could be damaged, or put her life at risk.

"Wow, this place is huge."

"Now close your eyes, and just imagine what a bit of time and love could do to this place."

She closed her eyes like he asked her, and he watched as her mouth opened slightly, seconds later so did her eyes. "Wow. This is like a blank canvas."

"We can do whatever we want with this place. I know some people would love to have a pre-made place. But this, come on, Natalie, see the potential here." He moved away from the door, through to the sitting room. "A huge television here, and there's even space for a fire so during those cold winter months you can snuggle up in front of it." He took her hand, being careful as he led her through to the large dining room. "The guys and all the old ladies around here for Christmas. I know Lexie is getting tired of the constant cooking and cleanup, and not everyone wants to spend it at the clubhouse." Next, he led her through to the large kitchen. "It needs to have everything installed, I get that, but look at it, Nat. We've not even gotten upstairs yet."

"Why haven't you started on it? I see your excitement, and this place is going to take some time to get up to code."

He took her hand, pressing kisses against her knuckles. "I want you to help me. I want you to design this house exactly how you see it being."

"Slash?"

"I trust you, okay. I know you won't do something garish with it. Your clothes are amazing."

"They're clothes."

"You're telling me you're not up to the challenge of making this place perfect?" He waited, and he saw her caving.

"I'll do it."

"Yes."

"You're going to need a lot of help, though."

"I don't care."

"You're sure you trust me with this?"

He cupped her face, careful as he did so. Her face was still badly bruised. "If I didn't trust you, Natalie, you wouldn't be here, and I wouldn't have asked. You can do this. Take photos and it can be in your file thing that I've seen."

"My portfolio?"

"Yes, that's it."

"Okay, fine, you've got yourself a deal."

She rubbed her hands together. "What cost are we talking?"

"Money is not a problem, but I have one condition," he said.

"What is it?"

"I want you to make this home as if it was your own. This is your project, your home, and your dream place to live." He held his hand up when she wanted to protest. "I'm the boss here, missy. You'll do as I say."

She rolled her eyes, which he adored. She always looked so cute when she did it. "I want to get started right away."

"I don't mind."

This was a project he hoped would inspire her, but also bring them both together.

Chapter Six

It took several weeks for the bruising on her face to go down. During that time, Natalie stayed close to home helping with the kids, still running through designs, or accepting deliveries to make sure the standard of clothing was perfect. They didn't want to sell clothes that were incorrectly stitched, or not up to their quality control.

When she wasn't at home with Devil, Lexie, and the kids, she was with Slash at his home. He'd walk with her as she moved from room to room, taking measurements. At her request, he already had someone working on the top floors. They were putting the walls together, fixing the wiring, and also updating the plumbing. The bedrooms and bathrooms were all a perfect size, so she didn't see a reason to change anything. While they did that, she focused on the downstairs.

For the longest time, she stared at the layout, wondering if there was anything that could be changed. She wasn't sure if the dining room and kitchen needed to become one room. The builder told her the wall between them wasn't a supporting wall, so checking with Slash first, the wall was coming out.

She loved the idea of a kitchen and dining room being all one room. That way the cook got a chance to be part of it all, even if she or he looked a little put out by the meal they were preparing. It didn't matter, really. The moment the wall was gone, she loved it and could already see the large table she'd spotted online in the space.

"This is what you've been up to."

They were into their first month when Dime,

Reese, Charlie, Pussy, Devil, and Dick turned up. It was Devil that spoke.

She smiled up at them.

Slash came out of the kitchen where he'd been pulling out old units. They had a large dumpster out back where a lot of the crap was going.

"What are you guys doing here?" Slash asked. He walked up to Devil, shaking his hand.

Staring down his back, Natalie bit her lip. He wasn't wearing a shirt, and a sheen of sweat coated the back. It wasn't just that, his muscles seemed to bulge, and his ink made him look so fucking hot.

Once again, her body was on fire, and she quickly averted her gaze, and focused on the book in front of her. She'd finished on the rough sketch of the kitchen, and how she wanted it. She'd also completed the dining area, study, and only had a couple more rooms to finish.

Yeah, so stop drooling over him.

You've got work to do.

"Nat, you want to come, show them around?"

She nodded, even as her cheeks heated. Avoiding the gazes of the other men, she followed close behind Slash, feeling like she was going insane as he smelled good, too.

Get a grip.

Slash showed the guys what they were doing, and how they were bringing it up to speed.

Devil put his jacket on the makeshift table at the same time Dick brought in his tool kit. He'd been known for making repairs on Martha's ranch as his woman liked to brag about his mad skills.

"We're here to help. You should have asked us some time ago. We're all in this together, remember?"

Natalie giggled. "Actually, we were going to get all of the main work done, then get your guys' help."

Slash gave her shoulder a comforting squeeze. "She didn't feel comfortable asking you guys for too much help."

"Please, Natalie, you know we're your slaves," Dime said, giving her a wink. She rolled her eyes. Whenever he was at the shop, he complained at lifting a box.

"I'll believe you like hard work when I see it."

She left them to it, heading back to her sketches. Her body had finally healed by resting over the past month. Lexie and Devil made sure she didn't do any heavy lifting, or strenuous work. There were times she wondered why they hired her at all. They took care of their kids without any help at all. She didn't mind. Being with them made her feel part of it all. If there was anything she missed, it was that feeling of being part of a family. She always missed her parents.

Finishing the final sketches, she found Slash still in the kitchen. She paused once again as he had an old fridge, which he was pulling out of the door.

Don't make a sound.

Don't say anything.

He looked … hot. Not just warm hot either. No, she was starting to really like a man with muscles. They caught her eye every single time.

"What's up, babe?" he asked, coming back into the kitchen.

She handed him the book and waited as he looked over every single page. He didn't say anything for the longest time, and after he'd finished the last page, she was nervous. Did he like it?

"I need to get my act together, and make this shit real, don't I?"

"You like it."

"Love it."

She gave a little squeal, and threw herself into his arms. Her ribs were all fixed up, but that didn't matter, Slash was always careful with her.

He gave her a little twirl, and she wrapped her arms around his neck.

Staring into his eyes, Natalie felt herself falling. Her body catching alight as he held her so tightly.

Neither of them spoke, and his breath fanned her face, making her think of his lips on hers. She'd not been able to enjoy his last kiss, but everything was different now.

She felt differently.

Slowly, he leaned in close, and she was so sure his lips would touch hers, but they didn't. Someone cleared their throat, and Slash pulled away.

Tugging down the edge of her shirt where it had rolled up, she looked up to see Dick. "Interrupting something?"

"Fuck off, Dick," Slash said.

"I fuck often, but the workers need refreshments, and I've been asked to obtain them."

"I'll go and grab some sodas."

She left the kitchen, heading outside to the cooler that she and Slash packed with food so they could work and eat on the job.

"Ignore him," Slash said, following her out.

"He's such a dick at times." She covered her mouth, and gasped. "I can't believe I said that."

"You're not the first woman to think it, and with Dick's track record, you won't be the last."

"It doesn't make it right."

"I've often wondered about him. The guys sent him because he was pissing them off. That's his talent."

She reached into the cooler, but Slash stopped her, grabbing hold of her arm and tugging her close.

There was a time she'd have been so pissed off by his manhandling, but right then a thrill went down her spine.

"What are you doing?"

"Every single time you look at me, Nat, it's like you're begging for my lips on you."

In response she licked her own, and heard him groan.

"You have no idea what you're doing to me."

"What am I doing to you?" she asked.

You're playing with fire right now.

She couldn't resist though.

Slash pressed her against the side of the car, and his hardened cock rubbed against her stomach. "That's what you do to me."

Natalie was a virgin. She'd not been with anyone else.

Being the tomboy, the little ranch worker, there hadn't been much time for her to experience stuff like that, nor had she wanted to.

His fingers cupped her neck with his thumbs underneath her chin tilting her head back so that she looked at him.

"You're the most beautiful woman in the world," he said.

"That's not possible."

"You're the most beautiful woman in my world, Nat. I love looking at you, I love being around you." His thumb stroked across her lip. "And if you gave me a chance, I could show you a life that you've only ever dreamed about. I could be your everything."

With no one to interrupt them, Slash slammed his lips down on hers, and Natalie melted. His lips were firm, but so fucking good.

She wrapped her arms around his neck, needing

him to be closer. She didn't want to let him go, or risk him pulling away.

One of his hands sank into her hair, releasing the pin that kept it at the back of her neck. His other ran down her body, cupping her ass and drawing her close to him.

He was twice the size of her, and even though she was a bigger woman, a size eighteen, he made her feel small.

"You feel so fucking good," he said, trailing a kiss to her neck.

She gasped as he sucked on her pulse, and her eyes closed. Every single part of her felt amazing, so alive, and she didn't want him to stop.

Her pussy was slick, and her nipples so tight.

Slash was the first one to pull away. "That's what you do to me, babe," he said.

He leaned down, grabbing several drinks out of the cooler.

What the hell had just happened?

****

Slash's dick was incredibly hard, but he ignored the slight pain as he took the sodas in to the guys, who were all pretending not to have noticed.

"I don't know if you know this, Slash, but the idea is not to suck the girl's face off. It's just to kiss." Dick then puckered his lips and started to make kissing sounds.

"It looked like you were eating her," Dime said, holding one hand out as he looked like he was eating something.

They wouldn't be his club brothers if they didn't ride his ass about something. "Fuck off."

"You and Natalie, is it the real deal?" Devil asked.

"To me it is, you know that. You don't have to go all Daddy on my ass. I have no intention of ever hurting her. She's safe with me."

"Butler told me what she said. I respect her even more now for not playing you both against each other," Devil said.

They all knew that Natalie wasn't like that. She didn't want to come between club members, and she was never seeking attention from anyone.

"Believe me, Butler is not cut up about it. He's balls deep in a club whore right now. He better be careful, otherwise one of them is going to slap on a daddy patch, and then he's royally screwed," Sexy said.

"Are you happy?" Devil asked.

The rest of the guys shut up.

"You know I am. Any news on the assholes who jumped her and John?"

John had stuck around because he didn't feel entirely safe at the moment. Slash had spent some time with him. He was a traveler, hard worker, but not a fighter.

"Nothing yet. There's been more attacks in the surrounding towns, but each time they're wearing fucking hoodies and shit. The MO is always the same. Unsuspecting victims, weak. They're doing it for kicks. Lola found the right camera, but again, we couldn't make anything out. However, we do know they filmed the attack. She's running through recently uploaded images on social media. She'll find them."

And when Lola did, he and the guys would pay them all a nice little visit.

He left the guys to fix the room, and found Natalie in the kitchen with a brush. She said as soon as the sketches were done, she wanted to get started with the cleaning.

By eight that night, a great deal of work had been done. Devil and the guys had already left, and he sat in the hallway, the cleanest part of the house, and shared a Chinese meal with Natalie.

He watched as she dug into her noodles. Her eyes closing every now and again. A little hum escaping her lips that seemed to go straight to his cock.

She tested him in every single way imaginable.

When she opened her eyes, her cheeks heated. "You can't keep doing that."

"Doing what?"

"Staring. It's not polite."

"I love watching you eat." He loved the way her lips pursed as she sucked up some noodles.

It made him think of how her lips would look wrapped around his cock, and those thoughts were not ideal right now.

"We're getting there," she said.

He was confused, and saw her looking up at the house. Damn, he thought she'd been talking about his dick.

Get your head out of the gutter!

Natalie wasn't like other women, and that was one of the things he loved about her.

"Now that Devil and the guys know about it they'll be more than willing to help. I wouldn't put it past him to round them all up, and make them come and fix it up."

She laughed along with him. "At times he does remind me a little of my dad. He's very protective. Not just of Lexie and his kids, but you guys as well. I believe he'd even die for you all."

"You're part of that as well, Nat. Don't think for a second you're not."

"It's not really the same though."

"You're part of our family, and he'd do everything in his power to protect you. That's the kind of guy Devil is. No one fucks with him and gets away with it. Those guys better hope that someone else finds them first because when Devil gets his hands on them, they won't live long enough to beg for forgiveness."

She nodded. "Is it wrong that I don't feel badly about that?"

"It's not wrong."

"John is scared."

"We're helping John."

She frowned. "What do you mean?"

"We're ... teaching him to protect himself. He's not a fighter, and he's been lucky not to get into one." He shrugged. "We're taking it upon ourselves to offer him some protection."

She giggled. "I bet he just loves that."

"He's not always happy, but he'll thank us for it the next time he's in a fight."

The giggle turned into a laugh, and it wasn't long before she was holding her stomach as if she couldn't contain her humor.

"What?" he asked, laughing along with her. "Okay, now I'm starting to think the joke is on me."

"It's just that..." More laughter. "I'm so sorry. John is like the only guy I can't see fighting. He's not got it in him."

Slash had to agree. The guy couldn't fight. "We'll sort him out. You'll see."

The laughter died, but during it, she'd gotten closer. His lips were so close to hers. He stroked her cheek, and the tension in the room mounted. He'd noticed that was happening a lot more now than before.

She licked her lips, and he groaned. "You really need to stop doing that."

"Why?"

"Do you really want to know?" he asked.

"I wouldn't have asked if I didn't."

"It makes me think of your lips wrapped around my dick." He ran his thumb across her lips, and slowly slipped it inside her mouth.

She didn't pull away or glare at him. Instead, she took his thumb and gave it a suck, making him moan. She teased her tongue across the tip, and then pulled away, her cheeks on fire, and she covered her face with her hands. "I'm sorry. I don't have a clue what I'm doing."

He took hold of her hands, and pulled her so that she was straddling his waist. The jeans she wore covered her pussy, but he still felt the heat between them.

"You're a virgin?"

Again, she went to cover her face, but he stopped her.

"You don't need to hide from me," he said.

"Yes, I am."

"I don't mind."

"Please, I'm like the world's oldest virgin."

"You're a little older than Paris."

She stared at him. "Does that make it better?"

"You're only in your twenties. There's plenty of time for everything." He ran his hands down her back, and when she didn't protest, he cupped her ass, squeezing the cheeks. She released a gasp. "You've not experimented once?"

"No."

"Do you want me to stop?"

"No."

"You'd tell me?"

"I wouldn't be here if I didn't want to." Her hands moved to his shoulders. "I like being with you,

Slash. I … I don't want you to hide from me either. I want you to be real with me. Don't be something you think I'm going to want."

Running one hand up her back, he cupped the back of her head, and pulled her close, taking possession of her lips while she moaned. Her hands cupped his face, as she kissed him back. She didn't fight him. She held him closer.

His cock pushed against the front of his jeans, and he wanted inside her.

"What changed?" he asked, breaking the kiss.

She panted, and rested her head against his. "I've always had a crush on you. After Dad died, and even before then, I was all over the place. I was scared, and nothing seemed to matter in that moment. Then of course Butler happened, and I didn't want to come between you, not once. I don't want to be the kind of woman the club hates. I've heard the way the guys talk, and they don't always have something flattering to say."

"You need to ignore them."

"They're your family, Slash. They want what is best for you. That can't be a woman who comes between two brothers."

He kissed her again, relishing her hands as they gripped his jacket. Did she even realize she was rubbing her pussy against him? If they didn't have any clothes on, she'd already be riding his dick.

"You're making it hard for a guy to play the gentleman."

"Then don't play the gentleman, Slash. Be yourself."

"And if you can't handle it?" he asked. He didn't want to lose her, not when he finally had her.

"Then I don't deserve you. You shouldn't pretend to be something you're not, not for any woman." She kissed him one more time. "Give me what you've got, and don't hold back."

Chapter Seven

Natalie walked into the kitchen, and paused when she saw Simon already at the kitchen counter. A notepad in front of him, pen in hand, she didn't even need to look over his shoulder to see another letter to Tabitha.

"Morning, sport," she said.

"Hey, Nat. Sleep well?"

"Yes, very well." She wasn't about to tell him that she'd had lots of sex dreams about Slash with his hands all over her body, making her take her clothes off, but doing it in such a way that meant she couldn't argue with him.

Her mind was sick.

The idea of being at Slash's mercy, of him being in control, turned her on.

"What are you doing?" she asked, pouring herself a coffee.

"Writing to Tabitha."

"You don't think this is a little much, writing to her every single day?"

"It's not every single day." Simon sighed and put his pen down. "Dad said a girl doesn't like a stalker, and I was being one."

She sipped at her black coffee and took a seat. "You don't look too sure about that."

"I looked up stalker in the dictionary and I'm not that. I care for Tabitha. I'll never hurt her and she likes getting my letters." He sighed. "It's useless." He dropped his head onto his hands, and she took another sip of her drink. "Dad won't move closer."

"His home is here in Piston County, honey."

"But Tabitha is in Fort Wills, and what if she finds someone else?"

"Then it wasn't meant to be."

He growled. "Why do people say that?"

Natalie stared at the young boy. "I used to feel like that," she said.

The glare on Simon's face began to fade.

"I'd get so angry. My mom, she'd tell me that in time I'd stop caring about wearing boys' clothing, and be more like a girl. I loved my mom so much, but I knew she wanted a little princess. You know, like Elizabeth. The kind of girl that liked wearing princess dresses, and being the fairy or the angel at Halloween." She chuckled. "I liked being the zombie at Halloween. Erm, I hated wearing dresses, and I would always mess mine up. Like I'd go out into the fields, and do some digging and they would be stained with grass, mud, and it was gross. I loved helping at the ranch when I was a kid. It wasn't my dream to own the ranch. The only thing I had that my mom also had a love of, was my drawing. She would get me to draw for hours and would put my pictures up everywhere."

"That has nothing to do with me and Tabitha."

"It doesn't. What I'm trying to say is only you really know how you feel about her, Simon. Be yourself. Don't try to be what other people make you. I've tried that, it doesn't work." She reached over, giving his hand a squeeze. "Don't hang out of trees taking her picture, because that really would make you a stalker."

This made Simon laugh, and she watched as he went back to writing his letter.

When Lexie came in, he was done and he left, giving his mom a kiss. "He's growing up way too fast."

"Tabitha is going to be one lucky lady," Natalie said. "I don't think I've ever seen a guy at such a young age be so committed and passionate about one person."

Lexie agreed. "Yeah, Devil is worried though.

They're kids, and they're already like this. What happens when they find someone else? Simon's a good-looking kid. Girls are going to be all over him."

"We'll see what happens. I don't think Simon's going to fall for just any girl. There's something special about Tabitha."

"She kicked him," Lexie said.

"What?"

"When they were younger. Simon's just a little older than Tabitha. He pushed her. When she got up, she didn't go tattle on him. She walked right up to him and kicked him. I think there was even a shove in there as well. From that moment on, they were best friends. Kind of weird."

"That's so incredibly cute."

"Yeah, I wish I'd been filming at the time. Tabitha is a firecracker and intelligent, as well. She knows how to wrap Tiny around her finger. She's also got a little of Tate's fire, but not her bitchiness. She'll make one hell of a daughter-in-law," Lexie said.

Devil groaned. "Please, all I need to do is hear those words, and I know we're talking about a Skulls kid."

"Simon's incredibly stubborn," Lexie said.

"He knows what he wants," Natalie said.

"Speaking of knowing what he wants, and completely changing the subject, are you sure you know what you want?" Devil asked, looking directly at her.

Her cheeks heated.

"Did I miss something?" Lexie asked.

"Besides the fact that our girl here is designing Slash's home for him, they also shared one hell of a kiss."

Devil winked at her.

She sighed. He was doing it on purpose to

embarrass her.

"You're not being very nice right now," she said.

"You kissed Slash?" Lexie asked. "When did this happen? I thought you weren't into him. Come on, girl, spill."

She'd never been one to talk about her feelings, and with Slash, it was so private. "I … erm… I…"

Devil chuckled.

"This isn't fair."

"I've been told a lot lately that life isn't fair, and Slash adores you."

"I like him a lot. Before everything went crazy, I would … ugh! I sound like a damn schoolgirl. Fine. I had a crush on him, and I would try to avoid him because he always made me tongue-tied. Now he doesn't, but he makes me … happy."

There was no way she was about to tell them that he made her horny. How she'd watch him from a hiding space in the barn, and that if he so much as looked her way, she'd get hot all over.

"I've got to head into the shop today," she said. "I've got to check over a couple of things."

She wanted to get away, and she wasn't ashamed to admit that was exactly what she was doing.

No one said anything as she left the house, which she was thankful for. Climbing behind the wheel, she released a breath and took off toward Piston County's main town. The moment she entered the shop, she stopped as Sasha and Pussy were locked in an embrace. There weren't any customers, and she found the couple sweet. She knew that quite a few of the brothers hadn't wanted Sasha as part of the club.

When Pussy first met Sasha she'd been blind, but it had been caused by a head injury from her stepfather pushing her down some stairs and banging her head. In some kind of reverse affect, she knocked her head again, and had been able to see. She'd already been married to Pussy and part of the club for several years.

"Morning," she said.

Sasha's cheeks were bright red. "Hey."

"How is everything?"

"It's slow at the home front, but I printed out all of our orders that we do directly from the shop." Sasha held up a stack of papers. Their online business was fulfilled by two places—directly from the warehouse if it was more than one item, or, if the order contained one item, they took it from the shop.

She took the papers and nodded. "I'll go and sort these."

"I didn't think you were coming in today."

"I have to check a few things out." She smiled at Pussy. "Having a nice day?"

"No offense, but it was a million times better before you arrived."

She laughed as Sasha hit his chest. "Ignore him."

"No worries."

Natalie left them alone, and rubbed at her chest. She didn't know why it hurt her to see the couple so happy and so in love. She loved knowing that relationships could work like that. Even her parents had one of those bonded loves that seemed to take over their life.

Entering the office, she took a seat at the desk, and caught sight of her reflection in the blank screen of the computer. Most of the bruising had faded, but there were still parts where it was a little darker. Under her chin, which from an odd angle just looked like she scraped it.

Rubbing at her eyes, she hadn't told Devil or anyone else that she struggled to sleep. She'd always wake up in a panic, and afterward sleeping was never an option, so she drew. Leaning back in the office chair, with Sasha and Pussy out front, she felt herself begin to relax, and then slowly fall into the land of bliss.

****

Slash was going to take her out to dinner. He'd seen Natalie in the dress she'd designed for herself, and it had been such a beautiful piece. She'd told him there wouldn't be an occasion or a time for her to wear it, but he intended to prove her fucking wrong. There was a time and he was about to provide the means.

Sasha and Pussy were cleaning up the shop as he entered.

"Where's Natalie?" he asked.

"She's back in the office," Pussy said. "Is she having trouble with anything?"

"What do you mean?"

"She's been asleep from the moment she went to that office. Not a peep, not even a movement," Sasha said.

"I'll go and check."

Leaving the two in the shop, he made his way toward the office and found Natalie with her feet resting on a stool, completely passed out. Closing the office door, he took a seat on the sofa and watched her.

He waited and decided if she didn't wake up before Pussy and Sasha had to leave, he'd wake her up.

Slash didn't have to wait long as she began to stir.

She opened her eyes and was instantly alert. "Slash," she said, frowning. She glanced toward the clock. "Crap."

"Sleeping on the job, not a very good thing to do."

"I'm so sorry. It's … I'm having trouble sleeping, and I guess I finally relaxed."

She pointed toward the door.

"You were able to relax knowing they were out front."

Natalie bit her lip and nodded.

"What about Devil? He's always home."

"He's always with Lexie. I guess I just … after the attack I've been feeling a little exposed."

"I'll talk to Devil."

"No, no, you don't need to do that."

"If he believed for a second that you didn't feel safe, then he'd be pissed. Don't worry. Nothing is going to happen."

She nodded, and he liked that she didn't continue to argue with him. "Why are you here?"

"Simple. I'm going to take you on a date."

She glanced down at her body then at his. "You're in a tux."

"Yes, and this is not one I wear for funerals." He made her laugh.

"I don't have anything to wear."

"Yes, you do." He moved toward the private wardrobe and held up the dress he knew was hers. "I want you to wear this for me."

"Slash?"

"Don't 'Slash' me. You know you want to and I'm determined to get you in that thing. I happen to have booked us a table at a really nice Chinese restaurant. I saw your appreciation of the food, and I'm not taking no for an answer." He still held the dress. "And you're also going to wear heels, and for once feel like a lady."

She shook her head, but stood up. "This is crazy."

"Please, Nat. Do this for me."

"You've already booked the table. You don't need to beg, even though you do it so prettily." She took the dress from him and he captured her chin, careful not to touch her bruise too roughly.

"You're worth begging for." With that, he dropped a kiss to her lips, and immediately pulled away. "You can get changed. I'll be waiting."

He'd wait for eternity for Natalie.

She wasn't the kind of woman to take that long though, and within twenty minutes her multi-colored hair, which still looked vibrant, was pinned up, and the dress she'd been saving hugged every single one of her luscious curves.

"You look stunning," he said.

Her hands ran down the sides of the dress. "You think so?"

He pulled her into his arms and placed his hand at the small of her back. "There's no woman more beautiful than you."

They left the shop together, Pussy giving him two thumbs up, and he gave him the finger. The other brother was known for saying inappropriate things at the wrong time.

"You brought your car?"

"I didn't think you'd appreciate the bike. I remembered how tight the dress was." And he'd imagined her in it a time or three.

Opening the door for her, he played the role of perfect gentleman, helping her inside.

He climbed behind the wheel and took them out of Piston County, into the city to enjoy some delicious Chinese food.

The restaurant he picked had a romantic feel, but also a relaxing one, and he felt that Natalie needed it. She'd been working hard even before the attack, and now it seemed to have messed with her mojo and he hated that.

The maître d' showed them to their table, where

Slash moved the man aside to hold out her chair. He was handed the wine menu and nodded at the maître d' to leave.

"This is really fancy," she said, leaning over the table to whisper. "Do you think we're underdressed?"

"Nope. I think we both look stunning."

She giggled and took a sip of her water. He ordered her a glass of wine, and himself a soda.

"Have you ever been taken out to dinner before?"

"Nope, Slash. You're my first one." Her cheeks heated, and she sighed. "Wow, I'm suddenly feeling really nervous."

"And you're talking more. I'm not going to complain."

"You like hearing me talk?"

"Who wouldn't?"

"I thought it was supposed to be some kind of thing where men hate women constantly babbling on about anything."

"I could hear you talk all day long."

She gasped, and he watched as her teeth sank into her bottom lip. "You always say something that takes me by surprise."

"And that's something I happen to enjoy doing. I don't want to be the same old boring guy."

"I like boring."

"No, you don't. If you liked boring, you would have stayed at the ranch. You may not like massive amounts of excitement, and by that I mean robbing a bank and car chases." He got another chuckle. "But you don't like boring." He saw the flush in her cheeks, and the way her chest rose and fell. "Far from it in fact."

"You consider yourself an expert at reading me?" she asked, tilting her head to the side.

He wondered if she even realized how sensual

she was being. The flirtation in her eyes, the promise of more. The dress she wore was so sheer that he saw the hardened buds of her nipples pressing against the front.

Slash had seen her when he first worked on the ranch. Whenever he went near her, she'd always freeze up or make an excuse to be anywhere but near him. He didn't take it personally, and figured she either had a crush on him, or she didn't like talking to men.

Seeing as she could talk to everyone else, he'd been instantly charmed by her crush. Of course, it hadn't taken him long to develop his own. The death of her family had put an obstacle in their path, not to mention Butler's interference, and that was all it was.

Just got for it. Don't hide.

"I consider myself an expert, yes." He leaned forward. He didn't want to break that air of sensuality around them. "Your nipples are rock-hard, and I bet they're begging to be sucked right now. Every now and again you stroke your neck over the pulse that I can see pounding against the side. You want my kiss, and then it makes me wonder if your pussy is as wet as I imagine." Her cheeks were on fire now. "And even as I say these things, you don't know whether to be outraged, turned on, or beg for me to keep going."

He pulled away as the waiter served them their drinks. Slash ordered their food, his gaze never once leaving Natalie.

She licked her lips, and he watched her take a sip of her water, leaving her wine.

"I've never done this before."

"What?"

"Been with anyone. I don't... I don't know the rules or what is expected of me," she said.

"Natalie, there's no rules. There never has been. All that there is, is you and me, and whatever we want to do."

She nodded.

"Tell me what you want, Natalie. I will try and make every single one of your dreams come true."

"I want … wow, this is so hard."

He reached across the table and took her hand. "I noticed you."

Her gaze once again landed on him. "What?"

"In the barn, where you'd try to hide from me. I noticed you. Whenever you walked around the ranch, I'd spot you from a mile away, and I'd have to stop just to watch you. You see, Natalie, when you noticed me, I already had noticed you, and nothing was ever going to come between us. Butler could try, but I wasn't giving up. If it wasn't for your father's death, I wouldn't have backed down." He locked their fingers together. "And this time, I'm not going to pretend to not look. I'm going to look. I'm going to see you, and I'm going to win you."

****

Butler sat at the bar in the Chaos Bleeds clubhouse, and he wasn't even pissed off about what happened with Slash and Natalie.

He wasn't mourning some great loss.

He simply didn't care.

Damn.

There was a moment when he thought his feelings for Natalie were the real deal. When he would have what other brothers had at the clubhouse.

"You're looking all down and fucking miserable," Dick said. He drank an orange soda, and looked way too perky for himself. The bastard was happily married to Martha, and they had a son. There were times that Butler had to remind himself that he'd actually seen Dick happy, and he even made his woman happy.

See, strange things did happen.

While Dick was a total bastard, he'd still found love, so maybe there was a chance for him.

Why was he so desperate to find someone to spend his life with? He didn't need it. Far from it, and even thinking about it pissed him off.

He didn't need to settle down. There was more than enough pussy to go around and they were pretty desperate for his cock.

But! He wasn't desperate for them.

The women he had fucked in the past few days hadn't meant anything to him. He'd not gotten the usual excitement or enjoyment at being balls deep within a woman. Instead, he'd been … bored.

He didn't even think it was possible for a guy to get bored, and yet he was living proof that they could. He didn't just want a woman that would spread her legs for anyone. The woman he was after was like the old ladies he'd come to respect and enjoy their company. The kind of women who you could leave in a room full of men and know they remained faithful.

He snorted to himself. The way he was thinking, he was starting to sound like one of those damn romance books.

"Now here comes trouble," Dick said, looking toward the door.

Butler turned his head, figuring he'd amuse his club brother, and paused. There stood Mandy. She had a bag on her shoulder, and even though she looked pale, she was still a beautiful woman.

She came toward them, and he admired the sway of her hips. Watching her, Butler thought about those plus-size beauties he couldn't help but admire. The women with the fuller bodies, ready to take on the world and looking ready for anything. That kind of woman always did it for him.

Even though he fucked the skinny chicks, the fuller ones always got his dick hard and ready. There was something about Mandy though. From the first moment he saw her, he'd been drawn to her green eyes. Not long after she turned up, Devil gave him the warning to stay away. Then of course, he'd turned his attention to Natalie, which had been a dick move if ever he thought of one.

"Do you know if Devil's in his office? I know it's a little late, but I need to talk to him," she said.

"You're in luck, princess, he's still there."

"Thank you."

Butler didn't even pretend not to follow her.

He stepped into Devil's office and found his Prez at his desk, pen in hand and a calculator on the desk.

"You don't knock?" he asked.

"Mandy's here to see you." Butler took a seat and watched as Mandy entered the room. She looked … vulnerable.

"What's up?"

"I was … erm, I was hoping I could have my job back."

Devil put the pen on the desk and stared at her. "You left without providing us any way of getting in touch with you. Mia has been worried sick about you, and you want me to rehire you?"

"My mother was just killed by my stepfather. I got the news … suddenly, and I didn't think to stick around."

Shit!

He saw Devil's hard-ass exterior break.

"I'm so sorry for your loss."

"I'd have been back sooner, but I had to be under police protection. They finally caught him, and I was able to lay my mother to rest. They have all the evidence to put him away. I promise I don't normally just up and leave like that. I would really like this job."

"It's yours," Devil said.

"Thank you."

"You start tomorrow, and I warn you, the guys will make sure the place is a mess."

She thanked Devil and left.

Butler stayed in his seat, staring at Devil. "You're a softie."

Devil got up from behind his desk, folded his arms, and glared at him. "You wanted me to tell her to fuck off?"

"No, but you're a man known for being an ass. For making the hard decisions, and you do. You punish the wicked and help the innocent."

"Fuck off, Butler." Devil stopped. "You know, I was going to lift your ban on pursuing the cleaner but seeing as she's all innocent, I may put Sexy and Guts on her."

Rage instantly consumed him. Sexy and Guts were known for screwing women together, not only that, they liked to do it on camera so they could watch.

"Don't forget who I am, Butler, or what I can do."

"You're a good Prez," Butler said. "I never disputed that."

"Then my advice, don't mistake compassion for a weakness. It's not."

Chapter Eight

Natalie's meal with Slash ended way too soon. She didn't want to go home, nor did she want him to leave. They left the restaurant, and once seated in the car, she turned toward him. "Don't take me home."

"Okay. Where would you like to go?" he asked.

"Your place."

She didn't have a clue what she was doing. All she knew was that she didn't want to go home, not right now. He'd weaved a spell over her so she was able to forget everything else, and she liked that.

He pulled away from the restaurant, and she held their leftovers in her lap. The scent of Chinese food filled the car.

His words kept repeating over and over in her head. The magnetism of his voice, the heat, everything.

She believed him when he said that he'd been watching her just as much as she did him.

What did it all mean though?

Neither of them spoke.

It wasn't an awkward silence.

The tension mounted between them so that by the time he pulled up outside of his home, she climbed out without his help, kicking off her heels and picking them up.

Slash rounded the car and pulled her into his arms, the glow of the moon shining down around them. His hands rested on the small of her back.

"I don't know what it is you want, Natalie," he said.

"I don't … I've … I loved this evening, Slash. I don't want it to end. I mean, I know it's going to and then we're going to have the usual after-date feel."

"Then how about I make a second date?" he asked.

"I'm listening?"

"Breakfast? I make a damn fine breakfast."

"And I'm really hungry. Like, totally starved. I mean, in the morning for breakfast." She was babbling, not making any sense at all.

One of his hands left her ass and cupped her cheek. "Breakfast is always a good place to start."

"I want this," she said, once again blurting words out.

"What do you want?"

"You. Your hands on my body. I don't know what I'm doing and I seem to keep saying that a lot and I'm probably driving you crazy with the same words and stuff. I really don't mean to be a p—"

He silenced her with his kiss. Holding their food in one hand, she wrapped her arms around his neck. The hand he had on her cheek moved down her back, splaying out and holding her tightly against him.

She gasped, and he plundered her mouth with his tongue.

"I will do whatever you want, baby. I won't push you. I'll give you whatever you need."

He suddenly held onto her hips, and staring into his eyes, she was overcome with need while everything became clear.

"I want you to touch me. I want to know what makes you feel good." He took her hand and led her into the house. The kitchen was only partly done. They still had to go shopping for appliances. The one room that was done was the main master bedroom.

She'd furnished it with a bed that was delivered, but she hadn't seen the final product, since she'd been sleeping in the shop.

Slash took her upstairs and she kept hold of his hand.

He opened the door and flicked on the light. The bed was huge, as she knew it was going to be.

Did she buy it with herself and Slash in mind?

She didn't know. He didn't close the door and she finally turned toward him.

He removed the tuxedo jacket and she stepped toward him. Reaching out, she began to unbutton his shirt. When the shirt was open, she ran her hands up his chest and pushed the shirt from his shoulders, watching as the fabric spilled to the floor.

Slash turned her, and eased the zipper of the dress down her body.

She closed her eyes, wishing she knew what was going on inside his head. The dress fell down at her feet, and she stepped out of it. Slash tugged her against him. Her ass nestled against his cock.

The hard length of him, pressed against her ass, and instant heat flooded her pussy.

"Just being with you like this has me hard, baby. You've always been able to do this. Even when you haven't given me the time of day."

He stroked up from her stomach to cup her tits. She wore a sheer lacy bra, which didn't have a whole lot of coverage.

"If you want me to stop, you've just got to say the word." He gripped the straps of her bra and began to tug them down until they fell to her elbows. He took the edge of the cups and eased them beneath her tits, before cupping her naked breasts in his hands.

"Oh, my," she said, leaning back.

Her eyes closed as he squeezed her tits before pinching her nipples, giving them a little tug.

The slight pain went straight between her legs,

and she dropped her head to his shoulder, amazed at the instant burn of pleasure from his touch. She already ached for more and she didn't want him to stop.

"I love your tits. They're so big and ripe." He pressed them together before lifting them up.

She finally opened her eyes and tilted her head a little to look at him.

One of his hands began to travel down her stomach. She didn't look away even as he teased the waistband of her panties. He stroked a finger across the edge and she licked her lips. Already her body was on fire from his touch alone.

His cock pulsed against her ass, and his breath fanned her ear. In one tug, he tore the panties and threw them to the floor. His strength shocked and aroused her.

He cupped her pussy, sliding a finger between her slit, stroking her.

"Now that's a surprise I'm delighted to feel. You're so wet for me." He teased down, and she tensed up as he stroked around her entrance. "My little virgin woman." He pulled his finger up and teased her clit.

She stared into his eyes as he played with her body. She was merely the vessel for both of their pleasure as he took charge, teasing her pussy.

All of a sudden, he stopped, pulling away from her.

He spun her around and sank his fingers into her hair, tugging her close seconds before slamming his lips down on hers. She didn't protest as he demanded her submission. He moved them back, and only when her legs hit the edge of the mattress did he break the kiss, pushing her down on the bed.

She gasped as he spread her legs open.

"Now you've got the prettiest pussy I've ever seen." He knelt on the floor and she went up on her elbows to watch him.

Slash ran his hands up her thighs, spreading the lips of her sex open, making her cry out as his tongue teased over her clit.

He slid down, teasing across her entrance, making the same movements as his fingers had done seconds earlier.

She was a virgin. She'd never done this with anyone else, and she didn't imagine for a second she ever would. This was completely out of her comfort zone, and yet at the same time, with Slash, it was so right.

He didn't make her nervous.

He aroused her, filled her with fire and burning need.

She'd simply pushed all of those feelings aside to deal with her own grief. There was no way she could hide from that anymore. He sucked on her clit, and she screamed his name as pleasure washed over every single inch of her.

Slash didn't give up. He kept on licking, sucking, and teasing her.

The arousal kept building to the point that she thought she might die if he didn't do something soon. But she didn't.

He hurtled her over the edge, and she screamed as her orgasm consumed her. She couldn't think or focus, the pleasure taking her to a whole new level. Something filled with hot fire and burning need.

She didn't want to give it up, or stop it.

The passion unlike anything she'd ever experienced before in her life.

Slowly, with his tongue, he brought her back down, and when she stared at him, she shook a little.

"That was the most beautiful thing I've ever seen," he said.

She licked her lips, unsure what to say.

"You're so fucking beautiful." He stroked her thighs and finally stood.

Natalie had no words. She was still reeling from her orgasm.

Her gaze on Slash, she couldn't look away as he rid himself of the shoes, and finally the pants. His cock pressed against the front of his black boxer briefs. She'd felt him against her, and in her hand, but that was nothing compared to finally seeing him.

The boxers went and he was as naked as she was.

He wrapped his fingers around his length and she sat up, reaching out and curling her own fingers around his.

Slash released his cock so that her hand covered his dick. Then his touch landed on her hand, and he showed her what he liked. How tightly he liked her to squeeze and move up and down his length.

She was completely enraptured by his touch. She went from looking at his face to staring at his cock.

The pleasure on his face was from what she was doing, and when she finally knew how to touch him, he let go.

She set the pace that he liked, and even though she was a virgin, it didn't mean she hadn't read or watched what came next.

Natalie wanted to taste him the way he had her.

Closing the distance between them, she stroked her tongue across the tip, tasting his pre-cum that spilled out of the head.

She released a little moan, discovering she didn't mind his salty sweet flavor, and covered the entire head of his cock.

****

Heaven.

Slash was in heaven. There was no other word for it. Natalie's mouth was perfect even if she was a little nervous at first and her actions unpracticed. No other man had touched those lips, licked her pussy, or fucked her.

He was completely new to her, and even though he shouldn't be happy about that, since he'd been with other women, he was. Slash ran his fingers through her hair, removing the clip that wrapped her hair up.

Wrapping her strands around his wrist, he stroked her cheek, watching as she sucked him. Where her lips were, there was a trail of saliva that she sucked on. She took a great deal of him to the back of her throat, but no more, and he didn't rush her.

The need to hold her head and fuck her mouth was there, but he held himself back. Closing his eyes, he counted to ten until he had control, and watched her once more. She looked so perfect, so beautiful.

She was his angel.

His woman.

And he was going to spend the rest of his life with her.

There was no doubt in his mind. He loved her more than anything in the world and had for some time now.

He was a patient man—or at least when it came her, he would be.

She moaned and pulled off his cock, running her hand through his pre-cum and her saliva as she worked the tip.

"Am I doing it right?"

"You're doing everything right."

Natalie took his cock back into her mouth, and he hissed as her teeth moved along his length. He didn't mind some teeth and he nearly rolled his eyes in the back of his head when she cupped his balls, squeezing them.

The sounds she made only heightened his arousal, the taste of her still on his tongue.

He wanted her again.

She didn't let up sucking his cock, and he watched as her gaze fell on him. She pulled off his dick and her tongue licked across the slit before sliding down across the vein at the side of his cock.

"Fuck, baby, you're going to have to stop. A man only has so much control." She was testing his to the limit.

Natalie pulled away, licking her lips as she leaned back. She really was the most beautiful woman in the world to him and having her in his bed was a dream come true for him.

Cupping her face, he helped her to her feet, claiming her lips once again. She melted against him, moaning as his tongue plundered into her mouth. He loved hearing what he was doing to her and didn't want her to stop.

She was everything to him.

Taking her hand, he moved toward the edge of the bed and sat down. He reached into the nightstand drawer and removed a condom, tearing into the wrapper and rolling the latex down his length.

Her gaze was still on him as he settled into the bed.

"Come here, Natalie," he said.

She climbed onto the bed, and he positioned her so that she straddled his lap. "What's going on?"

"I know this is your first time, and I don't want to ruin this for you. You're going to be the one in charge." He ran his hands up and down her thighs, relishing the touch and feel of her in his grip. "You'll take how much you want and you'll fuck me."

"I don't think that is how it's supposed to go."

"Baby, I can't hurt you. I don't want to. This way, you're the one in control. I'm at your mercy and you say what goes." Her hand pressed against his chest, right over his heart. "You feel that? It's what you do to me. There's no one else I care about. Only you."

She leaned forward, kissing him. "I love it when your lips are on mine."

"I'll kiss you every single chance I get."

She ran her hands up his chest, wrapping them around his neck and deepening the kiss. Her tits smashed against his chest and he gripped her ass, feeling her against him, his cock so hard it was almost painful.

Natalie took her sweet time, and he didn't have a problem with that. When she was ready, he held his cock, and saw her cheeks were a beautiful red, her innocence really shining through.

Her teeth sank into her lip, and she slowly lowered herself on his cock. He felt the thin wall of her virginity give, and she cried out before collapsing over him, his cock filling her as she wrapped her arms around him.

That one cry would stay with him forever. He'd never wanted to cause her pain and hearing it on her lips hurt.

"Ouch," she said, whispering the word against his ear.

"I'm so sorry, baby." Maybe he was a coward, not being able to take her, but he'd rather it be this way where she held herself above him. He didn't move, and she stayed perfectly still.

He ran his hands up and down her back, patiently waiting, even as his dick pulsed inside her.

"Slash?"

"Yes."

"I'm not a virgin anymore." She pulled away, and the movement pushed his cock further inside her.

She didn't cry out this time.

No, a moan of pure pleasure spilled from her lips, and the feel of her cunt tightening around his dick was the best feeling in the fucking world.

Slowly, she began to lift up and slide back down on his dick. Up and down she went, taking him a little deeper each time. He watched his cock as she took him inside. Seeing and feeling her was the most exquisite kind of torture in the entire world.

"Oh, that feels so good."

He squeezed her ass and thrust up as she pushed down on his dick. They both cried out as the pleasure went to another level.

Releasing her ass, he placed one hand at her thigh, slowly stroking inside until he came to her pussy. Running his thumb across her clit, he watched as she came apart because of that bundle of nerves.

"Oh, fuck!"

He couldn't recall her ever swearing and as he continued to tease her pussy, she fucked him even harder, taking him deeper, but it wasn't enough.

"Please, Slash … fuck me!"

Gripping her hips, he turned them around so that he was above her this time. Holding her hands above her head, he began to drive inside her, going deeper than she'd taken him, but he saw the pleasure as it hurtled her toward another orgasm. Reaching between them, he held himself still, teasing her clit until she screamed his name as she reached her climax. He gritted his teeth as her cunt tightened around him, consuming them both.

He drove into her, feeling the beginning of his release begin to stir, and he fucked her harder. The bed hit the wall with the power of his thrusts.

Finally, he found his peak as she came once again.

He saw stars.

Her tight heat squeezed every little bit of cum from him, filling the condom.

When his orgasm finally ceased, he moved so that he didn't crush her, and cupped her face, stroking her cheek.

"That was amazing," she said.

He ran his thumb across her lip and knew he'd found his future. There hadn't been any doubt in his mind. This woman was his entire world.

"You're the one that is amazing."

She smiled, and it brought one to his own lips. Her hand stroked his side as he was still deep inside her.

"Do you think we can do it again?"

"I think we need to get you cleaned up, and wait to see if you feel sore." Yeah, he'd been reading romance books as well. He'd even done an internet search to find books with a virgin theme, so he had some idea of how to treat Natalie afterward.

Pulling out of her pussy, he stood at the side of the bed. "Don't go anywhere. I'll be back."

"Where am I going to go?" she asked, smiling so damn widely.

"You're cute when you're being a pain in the ass."

"And you love it."

He took a kiss and left, thankful the bedroom was complete with a master bath. Slash filled up the bathtub, being sure to add some salts. While the water was running, he removed the condom and winced when he caught sight of the smear of blood.

He'd been her first and he'd be her only.

Chapter Nine

Natalie was on cloud nine. Well, cloud nine, ten, and eleven. She couldn't stop smiling even as she sat at the clothing store with a bunch of teenagers trying on clothing. She hummed to herself as she made her sketches. This wasn't of any clothing, though. This was of Slash naked as he stood by the side of their bed.

She paused.

Their bed.

Ever since she'd given him her virginity, she'd spent quite a few nights there, and she loved every second of it. The house wasn't completed, nowhere near. They shared Chinese food or pizza, and often made love inside his room. He'd awakened her to a lot of joys, and she couldn't wait to learn more.

She loved it when she sucked his cock, and it was clearly too much for him to handle, and he had to get her to stop.

"You're very chirpy today," Judi said.

"I'm happy."

Judi chuckled. "You make it sound like you're not used to being chirpy or happy."

She paused in her drawing, and closed the book. Even though Judi was married to Ripper, and they had a couple of kids, she didn't want to share her man with anyone.

"I don't know. The past few months have been really hard. My parents each passing. It has been a long road. You know?"

"I don't imagine for a second it has been easy. You can keep humming away though. I don't have a problem hearing you. I take it things are going awesomely well with you and Slash?"

Again her smile brightened even more at the mention of her man's name. "I'm starting to feel like a crazy person."

"You're a woman in love. That's perfectly acceptable to be a little goofy."

Natalie tilted her head to the side. "Do you still get goofy over Ripper?" Her own parents had been in love, but she couldn't recall them ever being so crazy about each other. The stress of running the ranch always got in between love and romance.

"Of course. He always surprises me, and not necessarily with gifts either. Sometimes it's the little things that make me realize that he's totally in love with me." Judi finished serving a customer before coming back. "We've been together for some time now, and he put his life at risk being with me. Devil had claimed me as his daughter, and in club land, I was the princess in a way."

"I think you still are."

"I'm a little old to be a princess. Anyway, it doesn't matter. We're together, and he had to prove himself to his brothers, and I had to make it clear to Devil that I was in love with him. You'd think the love over time would fade, or get a little dull. It doesn't. Ripper has this way of reading me. If I'm not feeling great or it has been a real hard day, he'll put the kids to bed, and come down to the sitting room. He'll take the book I'm reading, and I'll lay between his legs as he reads it to me. He'll run me a bath, or make me a morning coffee, or even breakfast in bed. So yeah, I still get all goofy over Ripper."

Natalie saw the love shining in the woman's gaze.

"Did you hear that Mandy returned?" Judi asked.

"She did?"

"Yep. Devil wanted to know why she left. Turns

out her stepfather killed her mother."

"Oh, no, how horrible."

Judi nodded. "She was in witness protection until they caught him. Devil rehired her on the spot."

She thought about Butler.

Natalie hadn't talked to Mandy much. Just a brief hello in passing, but she'd been working with Lola on the computer when that happened. She'd heard about Butler's interest in the other woman, but hadn't seen it for herself yet.

There was no jealousy.

Butler was a friend, and she hoped that this was his chance to get what he wanted.

"Hello, princess," Ripper said, entering the shop.

Natalie saw several women turn to look at the handsome man.

He may be handsome, but he didn't hold a patch to her man.

"What are you doing here?" Judi asked, leaning over the counter to kiss him.

The way Ripper held his woman, no one could mistake his possessive thoughts. "I'm here to take you to lunch."

"I'm working."

"Go. I don't mind working on my own. We're not overly busy, and any e-mail orders can wait until you get back."

"You're sure?" Judi asked.

"I'm more than capable of running this place." She shooed them away. "Go, eat, have fun. Be merry and all that."

Judi laughed, and left the shop with the promise she'd be back soon.

For the next ten minutes, she had a steady flow of customers.

When there was a lull, she made her way around the store, putting clothes properly on the hangers, checking the fitting room for any debris. Some people were so dirty that it always amazed her how much mess they made in simply trying on clothes.

At the sound of the door opening, she turned and her heart began to pound, not in fear, but in excitement. Slash stood in front of it and she remembered the feel of his mouth on her pussy.

"Hey," she said.

"So, Ripper texted me to let me know you were alone, and at first I didn't think it was true. Then I figured you'd be hungry." He flicked the lock on the shop in place. "And then my dick started to get really fucking hard thinking about how good it would feel to have your pussy on it."

She really shouldn't be aroused by his dirty talk, but she loved it.

"Did you miss me?" she asked.

He chuckled. "Now you're just teasing me because you know I fucking did." He held up a brown bag from the diner. "I've gotten your favorite."

She didn't have a favorite, but compared to Slash, everything else would lose.

Moving toward him, the moment she was close enough, he reached for her, pulling her against him. His lips were on hers and she wasn't going to fight him, not even close.

"I think we should take this back to my office."

Her pussy was so wet her need for him went into overdrive. He didn't argue or complain.

She took his hand and opened the office. He placed the food on the filing cabinet and she turned to watch as he began to unbuckle his belt.

"Drop the jeans," he said.

Wriggling out of her jeans, she made sure to turn her ass toward him. He'd let slip his fascination with her ass and when they were alone, she always found a reason to bend over for him. She'd often hear him moan, and it wasn't long before he had her naked and was fucking her.

Not only was she making up for lost time with him, but he aroused her just by being near. The scent of him always started up a memory of his hands on her. She wanted him more than anything else in her life.

When he'd been on the ranch, she'd often fantasized about these moments.

Slash stepped forward and placed her hands on the desk. His hands skimmed across the lacy white panties she wore.

"You know, just seeing these reminds me that I'm the only cock you've ever had and I'm so fucking pleased about that." He cupped her pussy and she gasped. "That I'm going to be the only man that knows how damn fuckable you are. How perfect you are when you come, and how tight your cunt squeezes my dick when you're so close." He slipped a finger beneath the fabric, and she gasped as he plunged straight inside her. "Have you been thinking about me?"

"Yes."

"Good. I don't want you getting wet thinking about anyone else. This is my pussy and this dick is all yours, baby." He drew his finger out of her pussy and slid it up to stroke over her clit.

The lips of her pussy were already soaked through with her cream. She cried out as he pinched her nub and soothed it with his thumb.

He tore the panties from her body and she moaned. "I'm going to need to go shopping for some new pairs if you keep ruining them."

"Haven't you figured it out yet?" he asked, leaning over her. His teeth grazed over her pulse, making her moan. "I don't want you to have any."

She cried out as his cock filled her pussy. One of his hands was still teasing her clit, stroking her as he fucked her against the desk. She expected it to move, but it stayed in place and then she didn't want to think of the other old ladies as their men did exactly this.

Was she Slash's old lady?

Natalie didn't have time to think as he thrust inside her, going even deeper. The touch on her clit went from pain to pleasure as he pinched and teased her pussy. At the same time, he fucked her hard. The sounds of their moans and flesh hitting flesh echoed off the walls.

She was so close, and Slash kept her at the edge, refusing to let her come. Only when he was ready and he wanted her to come did he let her fall over the edge, her orgasm taking over as he filled the condom he wore.

He wrapped his arms around her. The pleasure slowly ebbed away from them.

"You know, I only came to bring you lunch."

She started to giggle. "You can bring me lunch any day you want."

****

Slash watched as Mandy took the last of her equipment out to her car. The club provided plenty of cleaning products, but she liked to have her own stuff on hand all the time. Sipping his beer, he saw Butler watching her. The brother couldn't tear his gaze away from Mandy's ass.

"You know, I respect Natalie a lot more for what she did," Devil said, surprising him.

"Holy shit, don't you know not to sneak up on someone?" Slash asked.

"Nah, it's boring. I've got to get my kicks some

way."

"What was that about Natalie?" he asked, putting his beer down as Devil joined him.

"When Butler decided to be a pain in the ass. She could have pitted you both against each other. Instead, she walked away, refusing to come between the two of you." Devil stretched out his legs. "Before coming here, I never thought I'd have any respect for women. They all seemed the same to me. Wanting to spread their legs for any man that said a kind word."

Slash chuckled. "Lexie was never like that."

"No, she wasn't." Devil sighed. "I could have totally lost her, you know. She was ... everything. I mean she stripped to take care of a kid that wasn't her own. What kind of woman does that?"

"A good woman," Pussy said.

"I'd say we've all become lucky bastards," Ripper said.

They were all together in the clubhouse because their women had demanded a girls night, so they were all taking care of the kids, who were upstairs. Slash had already seen the men with kids holding a white walkie-talkie thing in case their kids screamed or made a sound.

Devil had Simon taking care of the kids as well. He was old enough to keep an eye on them.

"Ned Walker's on his way here," Devil said. "He wants to talk."

"Wow, you told The Skulls?" Slash asked. Ned Walker was family to their friends, The Skulls. His daughter Eva married the Prez at the time, which was Tiny. In recent years, Tiny had handed over the gavel to Lash. So far, it had been a wise decision.

"The Skulls told me, or should I say, warned me," Devil said. "Never thought I'd see the day I was having a conversation with Lash. I always thought it was wrong when Tiny handed him the gavel. Kid was too young."

"But he's been able to handle the pressure that was clearly getting to Tiny," Pussy said. "He nearly started a war with us. That's not a bright idea."

Devil shrugged. "He was worried about his club and family. He also had his town to worry about. I don't agree with what he did, but I know his heart was in the right place."

"So why do I get the feeling Ned's not here for something friendly?" Slash asked.

They'd once had dealings with Ned. Since the shit hit the fan over the past few years, they'd gotten out of the drug and gun runs. Their businesses were legal, legit, and no one could touch them.

Even all the brothers in Piston County were clean. Several stints in rehab had done that. Any brother that didn't want to get clean ended up without a patch.

It was a hard decision to make, but one Slash respected Devil for making.

"Lash has struck a deal with the law."

"What?" Slash asked.

"You heard me. He's offering his club as a safehouse to women and children who face being hunted down."

That was a big step.

"Lash called me. Told me he struck a deal with Kelsey's ex about wiping the slate clean for The Skulls. They helped to get women and children from sticky situations, keep them safe, while the cops go in and do their business."

"The club agreed?" Pussy asked.

"It was a unanimous vote. Lash wouldn't take the deal without every single member of the club having a vote. They were done with the runs, like we were. Ned is pissed. I'm guessing he hoped the club would get back into business."

"Wow," Slash said. Ned Walker was a fierce son of a bitch. Not only did he deal in drugs and guns, but he was the notorious leader of the underground fighting ring that was known for being lethal.

"Tomorrow morning, I'm calling church before he gets here."

"You want us to vote?" Slash asked.

"I want you all to talk about it." Devil looked across the room, and Slash followed his gaze, catching sight of Simon holding Amelia.

He got up without another word.

Sipping at his drink, he thought about what Devil had just said.

For The Skulls to get out of the business and to move on, it was really something. They were going to be protectors of women and children. It seemed fitting. The Skulls protected each other and their own. When they were united as one, they were a deadly force. When Chaos Bleeds were with them, they were a fucking army.

"What do you think about that?" Pussy asked.

"I think it sounds fucking great," Ripper said.

"I've not been interested in transporting that shit. I've got Sasha and Shay to think about. I'm not going to leave them alone. No way in the world would I ever do that," Pussy said.

There was no doubt about it; Ned was going to be so pissed at them if they decided to take the same path as The Skulls.

Slash wondered if it was even possible. Could they really break away from their past and find a new path?

He thought about Natalie. She'd lost her family already. There was no one else for her, and she was alone.

Going out on the long rides was always a risk. The risk of getting caught, a rival gang wanting what you had, even the drop off was filled with risks. There were a hundred and one different ways shit could hit the fan and make a real mess.

He didn't want to be part of that anymore.

Natalie had awakened something inside him, and he refused to back down. She made him want everything he'd never wanted before.

A family.

A chance at a future.

A life with her.

It was all possible now and there was no way he'd ever put that at risk.

He loved her with all of his heart.

Out of the corner of his eye, he watched as Butler got up and made his way outside. He didn't feel guilty for what went down between Natalie and Butler, or even himself. Butler never wanted Natalie, he just couldn't have what he really wanted.

"You know, our women are totally talking about us right now," Pussy said.

Death smirked as he joined the table. "You always say that."

"Whenever Sasha tells me that they're going to have a girls night, I'm always extra special in bed. I give her the love treatment. I always know I'm going to come out on top."

Slash shook his head. "I'm sure they've got a million different things to talk about besides us."

"Then you're deluded, man. I know those women, and we're the best thing for them to talk about. Look at us, we're hot, deadly, dangerous, and what's more, we're fucking ace in bed. Well, I'm ace in bed. I don't know about you guys, but if they start giggling, we'll sure know who is a hit and who is not."

"I need another drink if I've got to listen to you brag all night."

****

"Thank you. I was just coming to get that," Mandy said, taking the bucket from Butler.

He didn't know what he was doing. Only that he wanted to say something.

She bent over and placed the bucket in the back of her truck. The angle of her ass got his dick all hard. Her curves were like a dream come true to him, and he was having a hard time focusing on anything else, especially something to say.

"You clean up well."

Mandy laughed. "I'm really pleased."

He was going to beat himself with a shovel. "Do you like cleaning?"

What the fuck, dude?

"I do, actually. There's something about getting a place sparkling clean. You guys sure know how to make a mess. I'm just pleased that Devil gave me my job back." She stood up and flicked some hair off her face.

"I'm really sorry about what happened to your mother."

He heard her quick indrawn breath.

"Thank you," she said. "We weren't really close, but I wouldn't have wanted her dead."

"I'm really sorry." He saw the guilt in her eyes. "It doesn't matter if we wanted it or not, it still hurts though, right?"

"Yeah, I think it hurts more because I knew he was dangerous. I didn't trust him. It's why I finally moved out. He gave me that creepy vibe." She forced a smile to her lips. "Thank you for bringing my bucket."

"Would you go out with me?" he asked, blurting

the words out.

"Go out with you?"

"Yes, you know, like on a date."

She looked toward the clubhouse. "You're allowed to do that?"

"Why wouldn't I be allowed to do that?" he asked.

"Isn't there some kind of law that states you can only date people within the club?"

He chuckled. "You've seen the old ladies. Until Devil claimed her, Lexie had nothing to do with the biker lifestyle. We can date civilians."

She nibbled her lip. "I'm not really looking for a date."

"As friends, then? Do you think you could do that?" he asked.

"Okay, as friends. I know there's a fair coming our way again at the end of the month. Celebrating the last days of summer as we head into fall. Would you like to go there? It's silly, but I really do love the fair."

"I do, as well. I love the big wheel thing."

She chucked. "Okay then."

He watched her climb into her truck and take off.

"Are you stalking me now?" Butler asked, turning to see Slash leaning against the door.

"Not at all. I was just wondering when you were going to get your head out of your ass and ask her."

"I was being respectful to Devil's wishes."

"Whatever. I know you, and we both know Devil. He puts things in motion to see if we want it enough. He's always going to put the club first. It's what he does, and a woman not fit to be an old lady, they're not what he wants for the club. I hope everything works out for you."

"Slash," he said, watching the other brother

pause. "You love her, don't you?" Butler knew he, himself, wasn't in love with Natalie. She was a great woman, a friend, but she didn't get the fire started inside him like he'd hoped. Every time he looked at Mandy, he couldn't tear his gaze away from her. He wanted her more than anything in the world.

"She's my everything, Butler. I'd die for her. I want her to be happy, and I know I'm the man to do it."

"Good. I'm happy for you."

Slash moved toward him, holding out his hand.

Butler took it and shook.

Any bad blood that had been between them was now behind them.

Chapter Ten

"I refuse to talk about our men," Judi said.

"We all know it's what they think we talk about," Lexie said. She made her way around the group, pouring out wine for the women that would drink it, and sodas or milk for those that couldn't.

Natalie knew that Lexie was breastfeeding and never drank while she did. She took the glass of wine for her.

"I can get you a soda if you want," Lexie said.

"Nah, I'll stick with the wine." She wasn't going to drink it, but this was her very first girls night, and Paris had warned her—it could get a little scary with the talk of their men.

"So, I think it's safe to say we're getting a new old lady in our group," Lexie said, taking a seat. She looked toward Natalie.

"I don't know," Natalie said.

"Come on. Everyone who looks at Slash can see that he loves you. Like a total puppy in love," Mia said.

"I'm with Mia on this. Slash is very much in love with you," Brianna said, clinking their glasses.

She took a deep breath and smiled. "I really hope you're right."

"So, when he asks you are you going to say yes?" Paris asked.

"Asks me what?"

"You know! If you will be his one and true old lady, to stand by his side, and all that stuff," Paris said.

"I hadn't thought about it, but there's no one else I'd rather be with." She thought about Slash, and every time he brought a smile to her lips. "I'm in love with him."

"Then, my sweet girl, it's only a matter of time before he declares himself your one and only," Lexie said.

She raised her glass as they took a sip.

"I take it Pussy decided to be extra special to you this time," Jessica asked.

Sasha went bright red. "The moment I told him we were planning a girls night, it was like a competition with him. He thinks we talk about their prowess in bed, and he's so good at it, it's impossible to tell him we don't."

"But we do talk about our men," Lola said. "Until you let spill, with a lot of drink I might add, just how much Pussy likes to win at being the better lover."

Lexie burst out laughing, taking a grape. "They don't realize this is just our time to torture them right. We get to have some fun, drink wine, or milk, or soda, and eat."

"And while we do this they get to watch the kids. It's all for a good cause," Judi said.

Natalie laughed along with them, but her thoughts were really on Slash. They hadn't spoken about the future or what she meant to him. Their time together was precious. Repairing and creating his home meant a great deal to her.

"How's everything going with you?" Lexie asked, looking toward Jessica.

"We're still trying for a baby. I think if we've not had any joy in a year, we're going to have to look at getting checked." Jessica shrugged.

Everyone stopped smiling as they saw the other woman's pain.

Lexie reached out, touching Jessica's hand. "You know we're all here for you, right?"

"I know. I know. I couldn't be without you guys."

"Damn straight," Mia said.

They all banded together like a family, offering Jessica comfort.

The rest of the night they drank, watched a movie, talked about Naked Fantasies and the girls there. Some of the old ladies didn't like that the club owned a strip club. Others didn't mind.

She'd never been to Naked Fantasies so she didn't have a clue what it was like.

By midnight, they were all settling down, crashing where they'd been sitting. Natalie curled up, thinking about Slash.

She fell asleep with thoughts of him in her mind.

****

"Did you have fun last night?" Slash asked.

He watched as Natalie looked over the menu. The instant Devil gathered the kids, Slash joined him, following him back to the house on his bike. Natalie had still been dressed in pajamas and a couple of the old ladies had looked a little worse for wear.

Natalie hadn't though.

"Yeah, I really did." She pushed some of her hair off her face, but it kept falling down.

Leaning across the table, he tucked it away for her, and her hair fell into place.

"So … just out of curiosity … what did you guys talk about?" he asked.

He wasn't believing Pussy for a second.

She giggled. "You know, they thought that your guys' egos were so big that all we could talk about was you. I can't believe they were right."

Slash rolled his eyes. "Mine's not."

Her giggle turned into full-out laughter. "It's fine. We didn't really talk about you or anything. Of course, Pussy was mentioned and how he always does something extra special in the bedroom. Besides that, we just had some fun. Watched movies. Gave Jessica our support, and I don't know, we just hung out, I think. A little like girls do in high school. Only we're not in high school. We're full-grown women. I loved it."

He took hold of her hands, locking their fingers together. "I missed you."

She stared at their hands for the longest time before finally looking up. "I missed you as well."

"I didn't just want to take you out for breakfast. I spoke with the guys and they reckon we can get the other rooms finished. How do you feel about some shopping?"

"I'm all for it. But don't you want to leave the other rooms blank?"

"I want to leave one room blank." One day he had plans to fill that room with their child. "The other room and bathroom I want to prepare. I also think we can order the sitting room furniture as well."

"I'm all for it," she said. "Expense?"

"Go for it. I'm not putting a cap on you. Buy what you like and what you see."

"Wow, you're going all out."

"This is going to be my house." He'd have said our house, but he didn't want to scare her off. "I don't believe in doing things by half."

They finished their food, and when they made it to Natalie's car, she went to climb behind the wheel, but he placed her in the passenger seat. "I'm doing all the driving."

"What? Seriously? Why are you driving?"

"Devil told me how dangerous you can be, and I want to get there in one piece."

"Yeah, and I also passed my test. Devil was talking about the first time, okay? I was … terrible. I'm not terrible now. I'm a very good driver."

Slash still shrugged. "I don't care. We'll get there in one piece and that's final."

He went to buckle her seat belt, but she took it from him with the cutest glare he'd ever seen. Even when she was semi-mad, he found her adorable.

"I can so drive."

"And you'll get to drive, but for now, it's not happening."

They drove toward the city and Slash smirked. "Are you going to be a baby?" he asked.

"I can drive. It took me a long time to learn, and I find this rather insulting. I used to drive my father's pieces of equipment."

"Yeah, and I bet no one was around to witness that either."

She rolled her eyes. "I don't want to argue. You can drive my car." She patted his thigh. "What did you and the guys do last night?"

"Talked, drank some beer, played some pool."

"Did you go to Naked Fantasies?" she asked.

He glanced over at her, and he saw her watching him in a kind of weird way. "No, why?"

"Do you ever go there?"

"Sometimes. Only for work. Why?"

She nibbled her lip and looked away. "Nothing."

"You brought it up, so it couldn't have been nothing."

"It's just … something we were all talking about last night, and I know it's a strip club and all that. I guess I was just thinking about … us."

He gripped the steering wheel tighter. "And?"

"And I was wondering what you expect from us. You and me." She tapped her chest. "I'm not making any sense. Are we just, you know, is it just sex, or is it something else, something more?"

"It's not just sex." His feelings for her went beyond sex.

"Well, I was then starting to wonder. Are we dating? Are you dating other people? Are you having sex with other women?"

"No, I'm not having sex with anyone else. You're the only one I'm interested in."

"You don't want me seeing other guys?"

"Hell, no. Natalie, we're dating. We're together. You're my old lady." There he'd said it. "That's how committed I am."

To be his old lady, it was the highest commitment he could give.

"You mean that."

He pulled over when he found a safe enough place to park before turning toward her. Reaching out, he cupped her face, pressing his lips against hers. "There's no one else in the world for me." He ran his thumb across her bottom lip. "When I'm at the strip club, I don't give a fuck what those women have on display. Even when you showed no signs of ever wanting me, I wanted you. I'm faithful to you and you only. There's no one else."

Tears filled her eyes.

"That was supposed to be romantic," he said.

She chuckled. "It was. Oh, my, that was so beautiful. I don't want anyone else. There never has been. I was a mess after my dad died. Then you wouldn't listen, and I felt trapped, and lost, and all over the place. Butler was just a friend. He didn't mean anything other than being a friend. I'm so sorry that I hurt you."

"You didn't hurt me, baby. You never could." He took possession of her lips, and she moaned. "You're mine, babe, for now, forever, and eternity, because if there's a heaven, I'm going to do everything I fucking can to get there to spend all of my life with you."

****

"Ned's coming here? Without any of The Skulls?" Lexie asked.

"That's what I've been told. I've already spoken to Lash and Tiny. They've brought me up to speed with what they're doing. The pact they've made." Devil watched as his wife paced the length of the kitchen. He'd given Simon some money to watch his brothers and sisters while they talked.

With Natalie out, it gave him privacy with Lexie anyway.

"What deal?"

"The deal he made with the law, babe. Protecting women. Going completely legit. Ned's not got any access to The Skulls. Their slate is completely wiped clean. They don't get into trouble, they help, and it clears everything up."

She stood before him with one of her hands resting on the counter, the other on her hip. From the moment he met her, he'd done nothing but get her pregnant. She was his woman. The love of his life. His very reason for even considering this.

"Is that what you want? You don't want to go on the road, do the dangerous runs? I was never an idiot, Devil. I knew what you did."

"Chaos Bleeds have done a great deal for Ned Walker. We've risked our lives, and lost guys of our own. I've put my men through everything. Made them get clean. Piston County is our home. There's nowhere else I want to be in this world, other than with you. There are other clubs out there. Guys who don't have a wife or kids, or do and don't give a shit. They just want what they want, without giving a fuck what that does. I'm going to put a vote to the club. We've been through thick and thin together. They want to run shit for Ned, they can, but they give up their patch."

He'd thought about it long and hard. Settling down was supposed to have made life easier, and now it was. Their legitimate business brought in decent money, more money than he even thought it would. Ned Walker could offer them a lot more, he knew that, but that money came with a price. Devil wasn't getting any younger. His son was getting older. Looking in Simon's eyes, he knew his boy was destined for a patch in the club. His loyalty knew no bounds. His love was there, and being a member was in his eyes. He had to admit, it was also in Tabitha's as well whenever he saw the girl.

In this very kitchen, he had seen the danger posed to his wife. That had been a big fucking wake-up call. The threat on the club and the problems they'd faced, even though he'd never stepped down, and he wouldn't, it still amazed him they got out of them. He was Devil, Prez of the Chaos Bleeds club, and he never backed down. He wasn't going to start now.

He was being smart and considering everyone else as he made this decision. Watching the men with their families, their loved ones, that risk was too high, too great, and he'd be damned if he made a decision that could ruin their lives.

"What do you do if they want it?" Lexie asked. "If they want to get back on the road and you're the only that doesn't?"

He saw her lips wobble as her fear built. His next words shocked him as it just reaffirmed what he already knew. His love of Lexie went beyond everything else. "If they all want to do the jobs for Ned Walker, there and then at the table, I will remove my jacket, leave the club, and no longer be the Prez of the Chaos Bleeds. I'll be your husband."

Tears fell down her cheeks. "You love the club."

He smiled, and pulled her into his arms. "But I love you more."

****

Church

Slash sat at his seat, his cell phone already with one of the Prospects outside. He didn't know if any of the new blood would last and he didn't really give a shit. Each Prospect had to be put through their paces to prove their loyalty to the club. No one wanted a weak asshole at their back who'd run at the first sight of trouble, especially not him.

Devil entered the room and took a seat, but didn't speak at all.

No one spoke as they entered Church, everyone knowing this was a really fucking important meeting for Devil to call it.

Natalie waited for him in his room, which she'd been cleaning up when he left her. Just the thought of her cleaning his stuff made him smile. He didn't really mind though. It gave her something to do rather than worry. He knew that all the old ladies worried when they were having these kinds of meetings.

They could make or break a club.

Decision time was always the worst.

When everyone was sitting down, Devil finally began to speak.

"I want to thank you all for coming. I know calling church this early is different for me, but I wanted to talk to you about something. As many of you know, Ned Walker will be arriving here soon. I've got it on good authority he's going to ask us to take a job." Devil stopped and gave them all time to think about what he'd just said. "You all know what that means. The risks, the dangers, the fun even. I've spoken to both Lash and Tiny of The Skulls. They've completely pulled out of any dealings with Walker. They're going legit, and not only that, they're going to be working in witness protection as muscle and help those that need it." Devil sat forward. "I brought you here because I'm done with the likes of Walker. Since we settled in Piston County, we planned on building a life. We planned on being straight with each other, here and now. I want you guys to vote. It has to be unanimous. If you want to work with Ned Walker, continue with the runs, that's great, and that is fine. I'm happy for you guys to do that."

"But?" Pussy asked.

"But right here, right now, I will remove my jacket, and I'll call to get my ink blacked out. I will step down as Prez."

There was uproar around the table.

"I'm giving it to you guys straight. I'm not manipulating you with this. Vincent can—"

Vincent cut him off. "Vincent won't be taking over or helping out. You go, I go. I'm done with all this shit. There's too many risks, and you know that when I was younger, and fucking stupid, I'd have done it. I've done my time. There's nothing in this world I'm willing to risk anymore."

"I don't want it," Pussy said. "Watching my girl that last time … she may have never woken up. I might have never seen her beautiful eyes again. Now she can see me. At times I'm a selfish bastard, but I'm not leaving Sasha and Shay. I'm done. I want nothing more to do with Ned, other than saying hey at the picnics." He slapped his hand on the table.

"Judi's been through enough. I'm not going to put her through any more hell for a kick. The risks are too high," Ripper said. "I'm done."

"I'm out," Slash said. "One day soon I want to ask Natalie to marry me, and I can't do that if I'm at risk of leaving her. I won't."

One by one, they all shook their heads.

"I don't have an old lady, and I'm not looking for one," Sexy said. "But I've stood by your side through everything, and I'm not going to back down now. Being on a drug or gun run never gave me my kicks. I did it because it got us money and, building this place, we needed it. Other than that, I never liked doing it."

"I don't want to do it," Butler and Dick said together.

"The drugs nearly ruined my life," Dick said, speaking up, and giving Butler the finger. "I'm not going to risk it. Not with Martha and my son. They've been my second chance, Devil."

He saw the emotion on Dick's face.

"So, we're all done. We're all in agreement?"

"We're all in agreement," Devil said.

"We are, and you better keep that jacket on. The only way you're getting out of being Prez is in a wooden box, and I don't think that shit will ever happen. You're immortal," Curse said.

They all burst out laughing.

The club was always united.

They were the Chaos Bleeds and nothing would ever get in their way.

Chapter Eleven

Ned's arrival

Natalie picked up the large trays filled with burgers and made her way outside to where Devil had set up the grill. It was Sunday afternoon, and all the guys were buzzing about something.

Happiness was in the air, and standing in the backyard of the clubhouse, she felt part of it all.

"Hello, baby," Slash said, kissing her neck and wrapping his arm around her waist at the same time. He pulled her against him, and she leaned back, loving the feel of his lips, even though she still held the burgers in her hands. "I've missed you."

"You saw me this morning."

"Wasn't the same."

"Hey, hey, watch the food," Devil said, taking the trays from her. "It would have been your ass on the line, Slash."

"Yeah, and everyone would want to beat the shit out of your ass," Pussy said, slapping Slash's behind.

"Dude, anyone tell you you're a little messed up in the head?" Slash said, rubbing his butt.

Natalie burst out laughing. She loved this club. They were all a family, and always together as a team.

"I think he's got a fascination with butts," she said.

"He's a fucking weirdo." Slash turned his attention back to her and smiled. "Now, where were we?"

When he went to kiss her, she took his hand, and pulled him away from all the people at the clubhouse. She rounded the building until she found a secluded spot.

Slash pressed her against the brick wall, cupping

her face as he kissed her.

Wrapping her arms around his neck, she moaned as one of his hands moved from her face, down to her hip, and around to her ass.

He'd begged her to wear a skirt that morning, and she'd given in to him. The skirt was a wraparound that fell to mid-calf. She didn't like exposing too much flesh.

"You look beautiful today." The hand on her ass squeezed and heat flooded her body. She wanted him more than anything else in the world.

Her pussy was already soaking wet.

"There's something I want to tell you," she said, placing a hand on his chest.

"There is?"

"Yes, and before you do anything that will make me forget, or want you even more, I'm going to tell you." She licked her lips, and took a deep breath. Never had she been so scared in her life, but she'd decided she was going to tell him. "I've never said this to anyone else before."

"I'm kind of scared, babe. That could be a lot of different things."

"It's not bad. Well, not completely bad. It depends on if you want to hear it or not, and I'm yammering away, so I will just spit it out." She took a deep breath, stared into his eyes, and told him. "I'm in love with you."

He didn't say anything.

In fact, he didn't even show any signs of having heard her, so she told him again. This time, he smiled, and she said again.

"I heard you the first time. You're in love with me?"

"Yes, which to me means a lot more than just love, because I love a lot of people. I love Lexie and

Devil, Simon, the whole of the club. But I'm not in love with anyone else but you. It's you I'm in love with." She cupped his face. "And I've spent way too long fighting it and I don't want to fight it. I'm kind of scared, actually. What if my being honest with you freaks you out?"

He slammed his lips down on hers, silencing her. His tongue plundered her mouth, and the hand at her ass gathered up the fabric of her skirt. The palm of his hand pressed against her pussy, and she cried out, which he swallowed so no one could hear.

"I love you, too," he said. "I'm in love with you, Natalie. There are not words strong enough, and I now know why the guys always struggle with telling their women their feelings." He slid a finger beneath the fabric of her panties, and she cried out as he teased across her clit.

The pleasure was instant, amazing, and driving her to reach for him. She unbuckled his belt, and pulled out his cock.

"Baby?"

"I want you to take me right here," she said. "Take what belongs to you. I'm all yours, Slash."

He lifted her up. His cock already rock hard, and slowly pulled her down onto his length.

They both cried out at the same time. She wrapped her legs around his waist, and he held her ass and began to slide deep inside her. The feel of him within her was amazing, and she kept her gaze on his, not wanting to let him go, not even for a second.

He held her tightly and fucked her against the wall. Their pleasure consuming both of them, as they swallowed each other's cries in heated kisses.

Slash reached between them, touching her clit, knowing at any moment, they could get caught, but didn't care. He wanted her to come all over his cock before he filled her with his cum.

They were fire together, and with a few strokes of her clit, she came. Her cunt clamped around his cock as he continued to thrust inside her.

His own release didn't take long, and as they came down from their peak, he kissed her lips, face, and neck, just wanting to touch every single part of her, and not let go.

"I love you, Slash," she said.

He was completely in love with her. "I want to take you back to our home, make love to you, and forget about Ned's arrival today."

She giggled. "Then you can think about what we can do after you've gotten business out of the way." She wasn't going to pull him away from the club, or try to change him. Slash was the man she loved, and when you love someone enough, you don't need to change them.

"I'm going to be thinking about you all day now."

"Good." She kissed him again, and he pulled out of her pussy. Her cheeks heated as she felt the heat of his cum sliding down her inner thighs.

She was about to make her escape, but Slash pulled a handkerchief from his back pocket. He lifted up her skirt and got her to hold it in place.

"Do I want to know why you have a handkerchief?"

"In all of those fancy romance novels you read, the hero always has a handkerchief. Normally to wipe away tears."

She giggled. "This is the X-rated version," she said.

He wiped away his cum, and she saw the heated gaze he gave her. Was he thinking the same thing she was? About one day being pregnant with his child?

She placed a hand on her stomach, and watched

his eyes flare, and knew they were.

One day they'd have a child.

First, she wanted to enjoy being with him.

Holding hands, they left their comfort, and rejoined the party just as Ned arrived with several of his fighting buddies.

She was more than aware of what Ned did. His business and name were legendary. He commanded respect from a lot of different places, and he liked that. Even being old, a grandpa, he still put the fear of death into everyone who opposed him.

"I've got to go," Slash said.

He kissed her, and Natalie watched him go. She'd finally told him her feelings, and rather than feeling afraid or worried, she felt … on top of the world.

****

"Are you for fucking real?" Ned Walker asked.

His face was a dark red and his anger palpable as he stared off with the Chaos Bleeds crew. They were all in church as Ned and Devil faced off.

Slash sat in his seat, wondering if the old guy was going to explode. He didn't look healthy, not at all. His thoughts kept returning to Natalie.

She'd told him she loved him, and he couldn't get over her precious smile or her beautiful words. Damn, he was going to marry that girl—he had the ring already. He'd picked out the ring before her father died, and had even asked for his permission to marry his daughter.

Arnold Pritchard had given him a letter not long after. He'd asked Slash to wait until she agreed to marry him before giving it to her, and that was what he intended to do.

"Be careful, Ned," Devil said. "We're friends here. Let's remain so."

"You're a bunch of fucking pussies, that's what

you are."

Devil stood up, slamming his hand down on the table. "And what you're doing is crossing the fucking line. This is my club, my boys, and you will treat them with respect, or I swear, Ned, I will forget that you're Tiny's father-in-law and dispense with you as quickly as I can."

Ned and Devil faced off, each one glaring at the other.

"You have other clubs to ask," Devil said. Each word pushed out through clenched teeth.

"They don't know how to keep their mouths shut, Devil. You, Lash … you're both making a big mistake."

"No, you're making a big mistake by not getting out when you can. You think you're invincible, is that it? My club, my men, my responsibility, and the decision was unanimous. We don't want to do any business with you."

"What about the rush? That excitement that keeps you riding?"

"What about a prison term?" Pussy said.

"Or your wife finding someone else because they've handed you a life sentence?" Death asked.

"Or they take your kids from you because you've been caught in possession, and you've been deemed not good enough to look after your own kids?" Ripper said. "You want me to look at Judi, and her to look into our empty nursery, all because you didn't go elsewhere?" Ripper looked toward Devil. "I will follow you wherever you are, Devil. I don't consider you a pussy, but a man I fucking respect and admire. This is about more than drugs and guns."

"This is about family," Dick said, speaking up. "This is our family. Fucked up as it may be. We've got each other's back, and Piston County is our home. This is where we're going to spend the rest of our life."

"And you're not going to tell us how to live it," Devil said. "There are plenty more clubs out there."

"And if you don't get offered any special deal, what then?" Ned asked.

"This isn't about taking any kind of deal," Devil said. "We know what The Skulls have done, and if we're offered, we'll take a vote. This was just to stay out of trouble, Ned. We've done our time on the road. We're moving on, and we suggest you do as well." Devil stood up, and held out his hand.

Slash wondered if Ned was going to be an asshole and walk away without shaking hands.

Everyone seemed to be holding their breath as slowly, Ned took Devil's hand and shook it.

Ned left first, leaving the club at the table.

"None of us want to leave," Sexy said. "Dick's right. This is our home. You guys are my family."

"I'm going to ask Natalie to marry me," Slash said.

He'd been at this table many times as a club brother said those exact same words, and they'd never meant anything to him, not really.

"You're ready for that?" Devil asked.

"She told me she loved me," Slash said. He knew he wore a goofy smile as he told the club, and he didn't care. "I love her more than anything in the world."

"You're everything she needs," Butler spoke up. He got up out of his seat and stood before Devil, holding out his hand. "If two old dudes can shake hands, it's got to be hot for two sexy ones to do it."

"I'm going to kick your ass," Devil said, but he was laughing.

Standing up, Slash shook Butler's hand. They were friends, club brothers, and they'd be united to the very end. Through thick and thin.

There was a sudden knock at the door. A loud, insistent knock.

No one ever interrupted meetings at the club.

It came again, and Devil sighed. "We done?"

"Yeah," everyone said.

"Come in." Devil yelled to be heard through the thick wooden door. Lola appeared, and she looked straight at Devil. "What is it?"

"Five men have just entered Naked Fantasies, wearing hoods."

"So?"

"John called from the back office. It's them. I got some sound on the images that you got me to install at the club, and they're bragging about the attacks that went down. They're laughing about taking out Natalie and John."

Slash was on his feet, along with the club.

"Wait," Devil said. "This is our bar. Slash, Sexy, Pussy, Ripper, and Dick, join me as we get our friends. I want you guys to stay. Enjoy the party. Let everyone know we're going to be back soon."

The moment he could leave, Slash was outside on his bike. He didn't bother with a helmet, and he gunned his machine toward the strip club they owned. It was already getting dark, which meant the club was about to get really fucking busy.

Devil rode up beside him, and together they led the way to Naked Fantasies.

They would follow Devil's lead like always, and he didn't have a problem with that.

Parking their bikes at the private area at the back. Pussy had the van ready to transport them out.

Devil took the lead as they entered the club. One of the strippers was already on stage, dancing her ass off.

She didn't wear a bra, only a pair of panties as she gave it her all. Men called for her to take everything off, but she ignored them, dancing to her own tune. He wasn't paying attention.

Slash had already seen the guys who were yelling a little louder than everyone else.

"I'm so sorry, sir. I've asked them to keep it down, but they just slapped my ass," Darla said. She was a single mom, struggling to make ends meet. After dropping out of high school, she wasn't qualified to do anything more than wait tables.

"Go and get yourself a drink, Darla. We'll handle this, okay?" Devil said.

The woman nodded and left.

Devil didn't waste any time. He made his way over to the table, leaning against the side of the private booth.

The men couldn't be older than twenty. Each one had an evil look in their eye. Slash had heard of gangs of kids attacking people and uploading it on social media for some fucked-up kicks, but seeing the men who hurt Natalie, he was fucking angry. He wanted to hurt them all.

"Hey, old man, get the fuck out of the way," one of them said.

"Do you even know who you're messing with right now?" another asked.

They were laughing.

"I heard a story about you," Devil said. "I heard you beat the shit out of a guy and his girl up near the movie park. That true?"

"Who wants to know?"

"A guy looking to get a job done. We want it messy," Devil said. "Heard you could make it as messy as possible."

Everyone turned to the guy sitting in the center. "Yeah, that was us. We don't like fat chicks, and any guy who dates a fat chick needs to get his head examined, so we made sure they learned their lesson."

Slash was going to make sure they learned theirs.

"I've got the details out in the back. Come on. Fifty big ones for you," Devil said.

The promise of money led them out to the car, when they were there, the guys were already waiting, knocking them out and stashing them in the truck.

"You ready for this?" Devil asked, looking at him.

"They hurt my woman, and I'm not going to let that stand. Not now, not ever."

The door was locked.

"Lola's waiting for us at the clubhouse," Pussy said. "Sinner's there with her."

"Let's do this," Slash said.

They rode out to the clubhouse, Pussy driving the truck. The men were still passed out when they arrived.

Lola wanted their IDs, and as they got them tied up, she checked to see who they were.

"They're runaways. They've been in the system for a long time, but were kicked out when they turned eighteen," she said.

"What do you want to do?" Devil asked, looking at Slash. "I've got no problem killing these fuckers for what they did to Natalie, but she's your woman. You get to make the final call."

Slash stared at the men. He'd killed a lot of people during his time. Killing each of these men and making them suffer would be so easy.

It would be fast, swift, and … he'd feel nothing. They meant nothing to him.

Thinking about Natalie's smiling face, her

beautiful eyes, and he just knew.

"Call the Sheriff," Slash said. "Let them know we've found the men responsible." He turned to Lola. "Make sure you can pin every single attack on all of these men, with no chance of them ever being able to strike a deal."

"Already on it."

The men looked at him in shock. "I know you think I should end their lives, but what would I tell Natalie? That she doesn't need to be afraid because they're dead? They're six feet under? I can do that for you guys, but I don't think that's going to help my woman. Telling her that they're locked up, that is what she'll need to hear." He turned toward Devil. "It's a new path. You just put Ned Walker on his ass and told him to get the fuck out. This is our new path, and killing these five men ... we may as well take the deal with him. Not going to happen."

"I've got no problem with those fuckers being in jail. I know for a fact we've got a few friends who would enjoy the company," Pussy said. "Besides, blood is a bitch to get out of clothes!"

The Sheriff was on his way, and Slash stared at the leader of the little group. Slowly, he came around and glared at Slash.

"What the fuck is this?" he asked.

"I just wanted to look you in the eye one final time, and let you know that the woman you beat up is mine." He wrapped his fingers around the man's neck and squeezed. "If you ever think of trying to hurt what is mine again, I'm going to keep you as my own little toy to use when I need it."

The Sheriff cleared his throat, and he let the man go.

The club brothers smirked. It would be a lot

harder to drop his Chaos side, but he had a long time to get used to it.

Chapter Twelve

One month later

Natalie didn't think the blindfold was necessary. She'd been working on this house for some time now, and today was the big reveal to her, but Slash wanted what he wanted, and she just had to wait to see what was going on.

"I've seen it all," she said.

"Not as a finished product you haven't. While you were working at the shop, the delivery came, and I was able to put everything in place." His hands on her waist felt so good that she couldn't argue.

The past month had been like walking on a cloud of happiness. The best news she heard was that the men who attacked her had been locked up and were heading straight to jail. They'd attacked a lot of innocent people, and the evidence against them had been so high that no one was willing to defend them—a first in Piston County. She wondered if that had something to do with the club, but didn't care. John left town not long after, and told her he was sorry that he couldn't do more to protect her.

She really didn't mind.

Her heart was with the man beside her.

She'd also had a long chat with Butler. Their friendship was back in place, he was asking her advice on how best to deal with his feelings for Mandy. Poor guy didn't know what to do.

As for her relationship with Slash, she'd moved in with him at the clubhouse while this place got finished. Devil was all for it, and she'd never been happier. She'd even gone and visited her parents at the cemetery to let them know the good news. She liked to think they were happy for her. In fact, so long as she was happy, she knew they would be, too.

Slash moved her over the threshold, and her heart sped up as they made their way further into the house. The scent of lemon wasn't overpowering, but refreshing.

"I'm so nervous," she said. "Does it look good?"

"You tell me." He removed the blindfold, and she blinked a few times as she got used to the lighting.

Looking around, she was captivated. The house was perfect. The windows had been replaced, letting so much light come through each room. The floors had been cleaned and treated. The walls had been fixed and covered in magnolia paint.

"Oh, wow," she said.

She moved from each room, seeing the personal finishing touches, and when she came to the dining room, she saw it was set up for a romantic meal.

"Slash?" she asked, turning to see him.

He was already on one knee behind her. She covered her mouth in shock as he held out a velvet box.

"Natalie Pritchard, loving you, being with you, knowing you, is the greatest gift I've ever had. You are the love of my life, and I'm hoping that in our new house we can build a family together. I chose you, and I really hope that you chose me." He reached into his jacket pocket, pulling out an envelope. "Before you give me your answer, read this."

She took the letter, turning it over.

She'd recognize her father's handwriting anywhere.

Tearing open the envelope, she started to read.

To my beautiful daughter,

Slash has just told me that he's in love with you, and at first, I was sad that I wouldn't be able to see my little girl walk down the aisle. Then I felt incredibly selfish because I know I've had you all to myself.

Sweet girl, I know losing me and your mother broke your heart, and you probably didn't know what to do for the longest time, but I want to say, you're not alone. Chaos Bleeds will take care of you, and when I look at Slash, I know he will take care of you. He will love you like a man should, and I gave him my blessing.

I hope in time you will love him as well. I know you've got the biggest crush on him. I've never seen you blush so much in my life, and it is a great joy to know that you're going to be happy. Leaving this world knowing that, is the greatest gift of all.

Don't hold back, Natalie.

Fight for what you want, and love every second of your life.

Love forever,

Your dad.

"Yes," she said, dropping the letter as she went to her knees. "Yes, yes, yes, yes." She cupped his face and kissed him deeply.

Slash wrapped his arms around her, hugging her close. "I'll love you for the rest of my life, Natalie. I'll be the husband you deserve, I promise."

"I don't care. I know you love me, and I love you, too, more than anything. You asked my father all that time ago?"

"I love you, baby. Always have, and nothing is ever going to change that." He stroked her cheek. "My life didn't have any real meaning until I met you. Then it was like I woke up, and I don't want to fall asleep again. This house, I bought it for us. This is our home, and you're my future."

She kissed him again, and laughed as happiness flooded her.

Her love for him went beyond everything else in

her life. This was where she wanted to be.

For a while after her father's death, she'd lost her way, but now she felt like she'd found herself and there was no turning back, not now.

"How soon do you want to get married?" she asked.

Slash held up his cell phone. "We can be married within a month at the clubhouse. I'm not flying to Vegas. You deserve more than that, baby. You deserve the wedding, the celebration."

He sank his fingers into her hair, kissing her possessively, and she relished every second of it. After they'd made love on the dining room floor, Slash still deep inside her, he made the call to Devil to organize a wedding for them as he couldn't wait another moment. The sooner he was married to this woman, the happier he would be.

****

"You feel like you're making a big mistake?" Butler asked.

Slash turned to the third club brother who'd come and asked him as he stood at the altar in the backyard of the Chaos Bleeds clubhouse.

Lexie and the other old ladies knew how to throw together a wedding on short notice. As promised, one month after his proposal, he was waiting for his bride to arrive. She'd spent the past month making her dress, and he'd not been allowed to see any of it.

The yard looked beautiful, and with the last of summer fading fast, he knew it wasn't going to be long before the first frost hit, not that he minded.

He had a lot of plans for keeping them both warm during the cold season ahead.

"Fuck off," Slash said.

"I'm just saying. You want me to take your

place?"

Slash growled at the brother. They had all done something similar to each of the brothers who were now married.

Resting his hands in front of him, he stared at the point where Natalie would arrive. Devil was going to be the one to walk her down the aisle. He knew without a doubt that Arnold wouldn't mind. Devil took his responsibilities seriously, and knowing he was willing to give him Natalie filled Slash with a sense of pride.

The music changed, and Lexie along with the other old ladies made their way toward him, letting him know any minute now his woman was about to take the next step. The Skulls had also made the trip and sat in the audience watching them. Simon and Tabitha were sitting together in the front row.

They were holding hands and looked so cute together, even as they were getting older.

Finally, he saw a vision in white, and his heart nearly stopped. She looked breathtaking. She didn't want a veil as she'd told him the moment she saw him, she didn't want anything between them. The dress she wore molded to her tits, and flared out at the hips. The simple white gown just enhanced her beauty. Her multi-colored hair had been dyed a deep brown, and he didn't care. All that mattered to him was his woman, and the smile she beamed his way as she walked toward him.

He stepped down the aisle, and took her from Devil.

"You take care of her now."

"With my life."

They stood before the priest, and his gaze stayed on her.

"I love you," she said, mouthing the words, and he did the same, holding her hands.

They said their vows, which they'd practiced together. By the time the priest told him they were man and wife, he didn't need any urging. He pulled his wife into his arms, kissing her deeply.

"This is the best day of my life," he said.

She giggled. "Really? Don't men usually hate this day?"

He stroked her cheek as everyone began to make preparations for the photographs. "For some men, maybe. For me, I've been waiting for this moment for a long time. This is the start of my life, seeing you come to me. Knowing my club Prez trusts me with your happiness, this is a dream come true for me."

"Come on, you two lovebirds," Lexie said. "It's time to capture that look on your face before he does something to annoy you."

They were both laughing as they were forced to pose for the camera. The two clubs took one together as well. All of the old ladies and kids were in another.

Simon and Tabitha got one taken together.

They danced and accepted congratulations from the club. Natalie didn't leave his side, and he kept his arm wrapped around her at all times.

"It's time to throw the bouquet," Lexie said.

"We're still doing that?" Natalie asked.

"Yes, of course. There's single women here, too, and it's a lot of fun."

"Two seconds," she said, kissing him on the lips.

He took her drink and made his way toward the single women. Even the kids had joined in, as well.

Sipping at his drink, he watched as Natalie turned her back to the group and threw the bouquet over her head.

Slash chuckled as the bouquet of flowers landed in Tabitha's arms. Simon fist pumped and rushed toward her.

"We've got to get married now," Simon said.

Tabitha laughed, and they both ran to their fathers, holding up the roses. "We've got to. We've got to."

Natalie came to him, wincing. "I think I just caused a little trouble."

"It's fine." He wrapped his arms around her. "I think it's time I took you home and carried you over the threshold."

"You don't think it's too early to leave?"

"Nah."

Devil and Tiny were talking with their kids, and everyone was having a great time.

No one would blame him for wanting to cut the celebrations short. The club would still be partying long into the night, but for him and his woman, it was time for their own special time.

Everyone cheered for them as he carried her to his car, both laughing and waving.

Just Married was printed on the back of the car, along with beer cans tied to the bumper. He'd have to clean everything up.

Climbing behind the wheel, he took her hand as he drove them home.

"I love you, Slash."

"I love you too, baby." He kissed her knuckles, knowing he was the luckiest man in the world.

Epilogue

Nine months later

"I hate you right now," Natalie said, gripping Slash's hand.

"I hate myself right now." He held his wife's hand and tried not to show that her grip was fucking hurting.

She wasn't the only Chaos Bleeds woman who was giving birth today. Snake and Jessica were in another room as she'd gone into labor. The two women had conceived around the same time. Their due dates on the same day, and they both had said they'd give birth at the same time as well. They called it female intuition.

He didn't think for a second it would come true, and yet here he stood, holding his wife's hand as his club brother did the same.

The whole of Chaos Bleeds was waiting for the news on the safe arrival of both babies, and the health of both mothers.

"One more push, Natalie. You're doing really well," the doctor said.

She sobbed and moaned. "I can't do another one. It hurts."

"I know, honey. Not much longer, I promise, and then you'll be wondering what all the fuss was about."

Natalie lifted up, squeezed Slash's hands, and screamed as she pushed down, and then he heard it.

The unmistakable sound of his little boy. They were having a baby boy, and Jessica and Snake were having a girl.

"Is he okay?" Natalie asked. She collapsed on the

bed, and he watched as the nurses cleaned up their baby and did whatever checks needed to be made. "Slash, is it taking too long?"

Suddenly the doctor turned, and in his arms, he had a wrapped bundle. Their son.

"Oh, my," Natalie said.

Their son was placed into her arms, and Slash felt love bloom inside his chest. This was their son. Their baby son that they'd made together.

"Look what we did, Slash," she said.

"He's so beautiful. He looks just like his mom," he said, reaching out to stroke his baby's cheek.

"Nah, he's handsome like his daddy," she said, leaning back. Tears filled her eyes. "I love you, Slash. I don't hate you at all. I love you more than anything else in the world."

He kissed her head. "We can't go through that again."

She laughed. "We'll see."

Lexie had warned him that even if the pain seemed to be getting too much, the moment the doctor handed your baby to you, everything faded away.

"Please, find out if Jessica is okay," she said.

"Can I show him off?" he asked.

Natalie handed over their son, and he made his way out toward the waiting room. Snake joined him seconds later.

"She okay?" Slash asked.

"Jessica is fine. It went perfectly."

Together, they made their way out to the waiting room to give the good news. Neither of them lingered, and as soon as they were able, he went back to his wife.

Placing their son on the bed, he wrapped his arms around her.

The love he had for his family was unlike

anything he'd ever felt.

He was the luckiest son of a bitch in the world.

The End

www.samcrescent.com

SAM CRESCENT

EVERNIGHT PUBLISHING ®

www.evernightpublishing.com

www.ingramcontent.com/pod-product-compliance
Lightning Source LLC
Chambersburg PA
CBHW022133170626
46808CB00002B/971